UNSOLVED!
II

MORE
FAMOUS
REAL-LIFE
MYSTERIES

UNSOLVED!

II

MORE FAMOUS REAL-LIFE MYSTERIES

GEORGE SULLIVAN

SCHOLASTIC INC.
New York Toronto London Auckland Sydney

No part of this publication may be reproduced in whole or in part, or stored in a retrieval system, or transmitted in any form or by any means, electronic, mechanical, photocopying, recording, or otherwise, without written permission of the publisher. For information regarding permission, write to Scholastic Inc., 555 Broadway, New York, NY 10012.

ISBN 0-590-20357-6

Copyright © 1995 by George Sullivan. All rights reserved. Published by Scholastic Inc.

12 11 10 9 8 7 6 5 4 3 2 1   5 6 7 8 9/9 0/0

Printed in the U.S.A.   01

First Scholastic printing, May 1995

Contents

UNSOLVED!

II

MORE
FAMOUS
REAL-LIFE
MYSTERIES

Introduction

Using underwater video cameras and sophisticated sonar instruments, a team of ocean explorers aboard a vessel named the *Deep See* found a World War II U.S. Navy torpedo bomber in 750 feet of water in the ocean off Fort Lauderdale, Florida. They stumbled upon the plane, a TBM Avenger, on May 8, 1991, while searching for sunken Spanish galleons laden with gold and silver. The plane had the number "28" stenciled on its tail.

Shortly after, they found a second plane, a duplicate of the first, then a third. "By the third one, we kind of looked at each other and started wondering what was going on," said Graham S. Hawkes, the British engineer who headed the search team. "People stopped taking rest periods and crowded around."

Within twenty-four hours, the ocean explorers had found five planes, all Avengers, within a one-mile circle. Eerie videotape pictures taken by underwater cameras show the planes sitting upright on the ocean floor, as if each had simply come in for a landing, almost in formation.

Four of the five planes are in excellent condition. Even the windshield glass and gun turrets are intact. The plane that is believed to be the flight leader is broken in half and lies a little farther to the west than the others.

No human remains were found on the planes. Four cockpit doors are open, which suggests that the pilots and other crew members the Avengers carried bailed out before ditching.

The Navy has no comment on the discovery of the planes. Apparently the aircraft are as much a puzzle to official Washington as they are to everyone else.

For the past half century or so, hundreds of planes and ships have disappeared in an area that is vaguely bounded by Miami, Bermuda, and Puerto Rico. The area is called "The Bermuda Triangle." Now five planes have been *discovered* there, and they are as much a mystery as any of those that are said to have vanished.

Indeed, those five Avengers parked side by side at the bottom of the Atlantic are one of the most baffling real-life mysteries to come along in years. They have everyone guessing.

This new book presents nine other unsolved mysteries, each just as baffling. One involves an outbreak of random poisonings that had the entire nation in turmoil a few years ago. Another tells of the very strange and untimely passing of an American president. There are puzzling murders and mysterious disappearances. All of the stories have one thing in common: like those five Avengers clustered on the ocean floor off the coast of Florida, each is a riddle waiting to be solved.

Murder at Random

On Wednesday morning, September 29, 1982, Adam Janus, a twenty-seven-year-old post-office worker, felt chest pains after driving a neighbor's daughter home from nursery school. He went to a kitchen cabinet in his suburban Chicago home, got out a bottle of Extra Strength Tylenol, a well-known painkiller, and took two capsules.

About an hour later, he became violently ill. He was rushed to Northwest Community Hospital, where he died before doctors could even determine what was causing his illness. "Nothing seemed to help," said Dr. Thomas Kim, the chief of the hospital's emergency team. "He suffered sudden death without warning. It was most unusual."

That same morning, Mary Kellerman, a twelve-year-old seventh-grader from Elk Grove Village, Illinois, swallowed two Extra Strength Tylenol capsules to ward off a cold that was beginning to bother her. Minutes later, she became critically ill. Before her family could do anything for her, Mary was dead.

On Wednesday evening, the relatives of Adam Janus, the postal worker who had died earlier in the day, gathered at his home to plan his funeral. Among them were Stanley Janus, Adam's twenty-five-year-old brother, and Stanley's wife, Theresa, who was 19. Neighbors arrived with coffee and cake and sought to comfort the grief-stricken couple. Stanley happened to notice the bottle of Extra Strength Tylenol that his brother had left in the kitchen and took at least one of the capsules to settle his nerves. His wife did the same.

Stanley soon became so ill that his relatives called an ambulance. By the time it arrived, Theresa was also violently ill. Stanley died that evening. Theresa died on Friday afternoon.

The very same evening the Januses were stricken, Paula Prince, thirty-five, a United Airlines flight attendant, arrived at Chicago's O'Hare International Airport on a flight from Las Vegas. On the way home to her apartment on North LaSalle Street, she stopped at a Walgreen's drugstore and picked up a bottle of Extra Strength Tylenol. Once home, she took two capsules as she was getting ready for bed.

"We knew Paula was supposed to fly out again on Thursday, so we didn't miss her," her sister, Carol, was later to recall. "But on Friday, when we couldn't locate her, we got concerned."

When Paula's sister and a friend went to Paula's apartment on Friday evening, they found her dead on the bathroom floor. An open bottle of Extra Strength Tylenol was on the bathroom sink.

By the end of the week, seven random victims, all residents of the Chicago area, had died mysterious deaths. Police were frantic. They had no witnesses. They had no suspects. They didn't even have a crime scene.

The link to Tylenol was first noted by a reporter for the City News Bureau in Chicago, who thought it was unusual that the name of the painkiller kept popping up in coroners' reports. He mentioned his finding to a deputy coroner who passed the information on to the police.

To check the Tylenol connection, police went to the home of Adam Janus and questioned neighbors. They found out that Stanley and Theresa Janus had taken Tylenol capsules from a bottle on the kitchen counter.

The bottle was taken to a laboratory, where the remaining capsules were analyzed. Four of them were found to contain cyanide, a deadly poison.

In Mary Kellerman's home in Elk Grove Village, police found a bottle containing fifty-one Extra Strength Tylenol capsules. Six of them had been laced with cyanide.

Much the same evidence turned up in Paula Prince's apartment. Police found the bottle of Extra Strength Tylenol capsules that she had purchased the night before she died. Four of the twenty-three capsules that remained in the bottle contained deadly cyanide.

Near panic gripped the area north and west of Chicago where the deaths had occurred. Police cruisers rolled through streets, their loudspeakers blaring warnings. Daily newspapers and the television nightly newscasts also sounded the alarm. It was the biggest consumer alert in history.

On Friday of that week, the Food and Drug Administration cautioned consumers to "avoid in prudence" bottles of Tylenol capsules. By that time, however, news of the killings had spread far and wide, and retailers had taken the product off of their shelves. It was almost impossible to buy Extra Strength Tylenol anywhere in Chicago or the city's suburbs and in many other parts of the United States as well.

McNeil Consumer Products, the Johnson & Johnson subsidiary that manufactures Tylenol, determined that all of the bottles containing the poison capsules had come from Lot No. MC2880. The company quickly recalled all bottles in that lot and sent out a half-million warning messages to doctors, hospitals, and drug distributors.

When the McNeil Company tested other samples from Lot No. MC2880, they found them to be pure. This confirmed what investigators had suspected, that the bottles of Tylenol had been tampered with after they had been shipped from the factory.

Officials of the Food & Drug Administration believed that the killer, after purchasing a bottle of Extra Strength Tylenol, had taken it home, taken the capsules apart one by one, poured out the medicine, and replaced it with the cyanide.

"Whoever filled the capsules with cyanide did an amateurish job," said Illinois Attorney General

Tyrone Fahner. "Some capsules weren't even rejoined properly."

The poisoner then drove out to Chicago's northern and western suburbs and stopped at several drug and food stores. In each, he slipped a number of capsules out of several bottles on the shelves and replaced them with the homemade poisoned ones. Investigators noted the bottles containing poisoned capsules were usually up front on the shelves, within easy reach of the next man, woman, or child. When opened, any bottle that contained capsules with cyanide gave off a telltale almond odor.

Psychologists and psychiatrists developed a psychological portrait of the killer. They theorized that he was probably a man in his late twenties or early thirties who they described as having a "borderline" personality. It was possible for him to live a sane and normal life, but there were periods he was plagued with doubts and fears. During such times, the slightest snub or offense, real or imagined, could cause him to lash out. "My guess," said one psychologist, "is that there are people around the killer right now who think that he is a little bit odd but certainly not a threat to their lives."

Another psychologist called the Tylenol killings a "remote control crime" and said the killer was "probably sitting back and admiring what he had done." The enormous amount of TV and newspaper coverage the crimes had received, said the psychologist, had undoubtedly served to boost the killer's sense of self-worth, allowing him to achieve recognition that he felt life had denied him.

Within a few days of the first deaths, what was called the "Tylenol Task Force" of more than a hundred local, state, and federal investigators was at work on the case. They established a Tylenol hot line and checked out many thousands of leads and questioned several hundred suspects. They sifted through airline, bus, and train records, hoping to determine if any of their suspects traveled to or from Chicago late in September 1982 when the poisoned capsules were planted.

Investigators worried that if they didn't catch the killer quickly, he would strike again. And he might not use Tylenol, but choose another product.

Authorities also feared an outbreak of "copycat" killings. Indeed, in the weeks following the newspaper headlines concerning the Tylenol case, scores of poison scares occurred all over the nation.

A break in the case seemed to have arrived late in 1982 when police caught thirty-six-year-old James Lewis, who was being sought for extortion in the case. Lewis was believed to have sent a handwritten letter to Johnson & Johnson demanding $1 million "to stop the killings."

The letter and the envelope in which it was contained had become the subject of an intense investigation. Since the envelope had a New York City postmark, it involved hundreds of New York City detectives and FBI agents. Through handwriting analysis, they were able to trace the letter to Lewis.

When detectives checked Lewis's background,

they learned he was wanted by postal inspectors for credit card fraud in Kansas City, Missouri. They also learned he had been charged with murder in Kansas City but had been freed on a legal technicality.

Lewis and his wife, LeAnn, left Kansas City for Chicago in December 1981, where Lewis got a job as a tax preparer and his wife went to work in a travel agency. The couple moved to New York early in September 1982, the same month the Tylenol killings took place.

Because investigators believed the Lewises were hiding in New York, they launched a large-scale hunt there. Lewis had mailed letters to the Chicago *Tribune* from New York in which he denied having any connection to the killings. Investigators reasoned that Lewis must have been reading the *Tribune* regularly to see whether his letters were being published. So they staked out newsstands in New York that carried out-of-town newspapers. And they put up posters of Lewis and his wife in libraries where out-of-town newspapers could be read. The posters asked people to call if they spotted either or both of the Lewises.

Eventually, someone did. On December 13, 1982, James Lewis was sitting at a long table in the Mid-Manhattan Branch of the New York Public Library, copying names and addresses of newspapers from a book, when a detective walked up behind him and tapped him on the shoulder. Lewis jumped to his feet. The detective flashed a badge and said, "Come with me." Lewis went quietly.

Mrs. Lewis surrendered to police in Chicago the day following her husband's arrest.

Lewis was also thought to have sent a letter to the White House in which he threatened the lives of President Ronald Reagan and others. In the letter, he was said to have referred to the Tylenol killings. "We have Lewis's handwriting in the death threat to the President," said U.S. Attorney Daniel K. Webb.

Lewis was returned to Kansas City where he was tried and convicted of credit card fraud and sentenced to ten years in prison. That was only the beginning. After being sentenced in Kansas City, Lewis was taken to Chicago and there tried for extortion in the Tylenol case. Found guilty, he received a second prison sentence of ten years. Lewis was made to serve his sentences in the federal prison in El Reno, Oklahoma.

From the beginning, Lewis denied he had any connection with the Tylenol killings. Investigators were never able to establish that he did. All Lewis really did was "piggyback" on the crime.

Other hopes for a solution also fizzled. Within six months after the crime, the number of investigators had been cut to thirty and the hot line had been disconnected. "We don't have any significant leads," said one investigator. "And we don't have any suspects. It's depressing." The $100,000 offered for the capture of the killer has never been claimed.

There is an interesting footnote to the Tylenol case. For Johnson & Johnson, in particular, and the food and drug industry, in general, the Tylenol tragedy marked the beginning of a long struggle to develop bottles, boxes, and other containers that are tamper-resistant. Companies both large and small have been affected.

One example of what has happened: Some pill and capsule manufacturers now package their products in "blister packs." These are plastic sheets in which each pill or capsule is tightly sealed in its own bubble. With a blister pack, any evidence of tampering clearly shows.

A wide range of food and grocery products are now sold in tamper-resistant packages. Tight plastic bands or plastic shrink wraps cover the necks of some syrup and sauce bottles, and baby food jars are fitted with "pop tops" that bulge noticeably once they've been opened. Other products are vacuum sealed, like cans of coffee, not merely to maintain freshness but as a guard against tampering. Greater packaging safety is a direct result of the Tylenol tragedy.

The Brief Life of
a Superhero

His name was Bruce Lee, but to his millions upon millions of fans around the globe he was known as The King of Kung Fu, The Fist That Shook the World, or The Man With the Golden Arm. In the space of two years during the early 1970's, he went from being relatively unknown to having the status of an international superstar, with the asking price of a million dollars a film.

He was a joy to watch on the screen. His kung fu style put the emphasis on speed — flying kicks and hands that moved quicker than the eye could follow. His grace was compared to that of a ballet star.

In his films, Bruce Lee played the role of a hero who, singlehandedly and against great odds, conquers evil opponents to restore peace and harmony to the world. About half of each of his films was made up of fight scenes, with his audiences cheering loudly each punch and kick.

Bruce Lee was youthful and refreshing, often even boyish on the screen. But in real life, his personality turned away as many people as he attracted. He could be self-centered and arrogant, a hothead with a quick temper. His work was what was important to him, and he had a sense of mission about it. Little else mattered.

In 1973, at the age of thirty-two, Bruce Lee was at his physical peak, when the news was flashed from Hong Kong, where he was working on a film, that he had died under mysterious circumstances. Investigations into his death seemed to contradict one another. At first, drugs were said to be a factor, then a puzzling brain injury. Even his unusual diet was given as a cause. Some believe that an exotic martial arts ritual brought about Bruce Lee's death.

In 1993, the Bruce Lee story took another bizarre turn when his twenty-eight-year-old son, Brandon Lee, also an actor, died a strange death on a movie set in North Carolina. His son's passing served to deepen the mystery surrounding Bruce Lee and add another dimension to the growing legend.

In 1939, Lee Hoi Chuen, a popular entertainer in China, brought his wife, Grace, the couple's son, Peter, and their two daughters, Agnes and Phoebe, from their home in Hong Kong to live in San Francisco, where he was appearing in a play. On November 27, 1940, while the family was still in San Francisco, another son was born. His mother wanted to name him Yuen Kam. But a nurse at the hospital decided the baby needed a simpler name and put Bruce on the child's birth certificate, and the parents let the name stand.

Before Bruce Lee was a year old, the family returned to Hong Kong. As a boy growing up, Bruce often visited his father on the sets of movies in which he was performing. One day when Bruce was six, the director of one of his father's films offered him a part in a movie called *The Beginning of a Boy*. Parts in other films quickly followed.

"Even at the age of seven, Lee's screen persona was strong," says one of his biographers. "He was a clever, capable, but short-tempered little ruffian who specialized in the scowl, the pout, the stare, and the slow burn."

To some extent, this was the character young Bruce was beginning to play in real life. He traveled with a gang and was beginning to earn a reputation as a street-fighting punk.

This led him to study kung fu, a Chinese art of self-defense somewhat the same as karate. Bruce felt that kung fu would help to make him a more efficient fighting machine.

As a teenager Bruce got into more and more fights. "Kids in Hong Kong have nothing to look forward to," Bruce once told a reporter. "The [British] white kids have all the best jobs and the rest of us had to work for them. That's why most kids become punks. Life in Hong Kong is so bad. Kids in slums can never get out."

In addition to kung fu, Bruce studied wing chun, a highly sophisticated Chinese self-defense system. He practiced long and hard until he became skilled in the art.

At the time, Bruce was attending St. Francis Xavier School in Hong Kong. One of his teachers, Brother Edward, noted that Bruce was becoming more and more reckless and violent. To take him down a peg, Brother Edward invited Bruce to go into the boxing room with him and put on the gloves in a friendly match. Bruce had never boxed in his life, but by using wing chun tactics he was able to hold his own against this bigger, more experienced opponent.

Brother Edward was so impressed he invited Bruce to join the boxing team. Not long after, in one of his first tournaments, Bruce defeated the boy who had been boxing champion three years in a row.

All the while, Bruce was continuing to make movies. In one, *The Orphan*, Bruce played a street punk who is involved in one street fight after another. Some of his critics said that his fight scenes were little more than carefully staged dance sequences. There is some truth in this, for in his early years Bruce learned all the popular dances. His favorite was the cha-cha, a Latin-American dance. In fact, Bruce was Hong Kong's cha-cha champion, winning many trophies.

By the time he was eighteen, Bruce had appeared in twenty films in Hong Kong under the name Lee Siu Loong, the Little Dragon, and his popularity was mushrooming. Run Run Shaw, a powerful film producer in Asia, offered him a contract. Bruce was thrilled. He told his mother he wanted to quit high school and accept Run Run Shaw's offer.

His mother said no. She wanted Bruce to finish school and get his diploma. She was also worried about all the street fighting he was doing. While she was trying to decide what to do, Bruce was picked up by the police for fighting. That was more than his mother could take. She made up her mind to send Bruce to live with friends in the United States, where he could finish high school and make something of his life.

In the United States, Bruce completed high school and went on to college at the University of Washington. He earned spending money by teaching kung fu. Swedish-born Linda Emery was one of his students. In 1964, they were married and, shortly after, moved to California. A son, Brandon, was born to the couple in 1965.

Bruce continued to polish his skills in the martial arts. He even created a personal system of kung fu. He called it jeet kune do — the way of the intercepting fist.

In jeet kune do, there were no colored belts and no formal bowing as in karate. A student was expected to create his own fighting style, using techniques from other martial arts.

Richard Goldstein, writing in *The Village Voice*, once described an incident that illustrated jeet kune do. It took place on a late-night talk show in Hong Kong. A panel of martial arts masters, including Bruce, were the invited guests. The most experienced of the masters invited the others to attempt to throw him. One by one, they tried. Each approached the master, bowed, and then attempted to knock him off his feet. Each failed. Then it was Bruce's turn. He got up and punched the master in the mouth. "You best believe he fell," said Goldstein.

Bruce began teaching jeet kune do to such Hollywood celebrities of the day as Steve McQueen and James Coburn. Bruce received as much as $250 an hour for a private lesson.

While he was successful as an instructor, Bruce's career in films was at a standstill, chiefly because there were so few parts in American movies for Asians. In 1966, Bruce landed the role of Kato in *The Green Hornet* television series. Similar to *Batman*, the series teamed the Green Hornet and his faithful valet and chauffeur Kato in a series of action-filled adventures in which they baffled assorted evildoers.

When the series was introduced, the Green Hornet himself, as the title character, was the star. But little by little, the emphasis shifted to Kato, and people began watching the series mainly because of Bruce. Looking young and clean-cut, he brought a sense of realism to his role, quickly finishing off any and all of the Green Hornet's opponents with simplicity and style. Unfortunately for Bruce, *The Green Hornet* lasted only one season on television.

After *The Green Hornet*, Bruce's career slumped for a while. He had a small part in *Marlowe*, a feature film starring James Garner. He also appeared in several episodes of *Longstreet*, a television series in which he taught James Franciscus how to fight.

Bruce was hoping to land the leading role in *Kung Fu*, a television series about a martial arts hero who travels the West overcoming bad guys with his wits and heavy doses of kung fu. But even though he had helped to develop the idea, Bruce was turned down for the leading role in favor of tall and lean David Carradine. Bruce was just as lean as Carradine, but not as tall. (Bruce, according to his wife, stood 5-foot 7½.)

And he was Asian. Bruce was convinced by now that his Asian features put a limit on his future in Hollywood.

Nevertheless, Bruce remained determined to become not merely a successful actor, but a star. With that as his goal, he and his family packed up and moved back to Hong Kong.

There Bruce teamed up with producer Raymond Chow, who wanted to make the first kung fu film in modern dress, one in which a real, modern-day Asian would fight with his feet. Audiences loved the film, which was titled *The Big Boss*. The film was released as *Fists of Fury* in the United States.

After the film had been released, Bruce would sometimes slip unnoticed into Hong Kong theaters to watch how the audience reacted. Because Hong Kong moviegoers see so many kung fu films, they don't get excited unless they're watching something special. But when they saw Bruce kicking and punching, the audience cheered, applauded wildly, and practically jumped out of their seats.

With the success of *The Big Boss* and the films that immediately followed, *The Chinese Connection* in 1972, and *Return of the Dragon* in 1973, Bruce became an Asian film star of the first rank. There were growing audiences for his films in Europe and North America as well. By this time, Bruce was not only starring in films, but involved in writing and directing as well.

Return of the Dragon, was marked by the appearance of Chuck Norris, the American karate champion. Bruce and Norris staged a fight scene in the Roman Coliseum at the end of the film that is now regarded as a classic. Norris downed Bruce, who recovered shakily. He then attacked Norris with a series of spin kicks, back kicks, and several other flashy moves. Norris went down, then got up, staggering, breathing heavily. Bruce looked at his opponent with a mixture of scorn and pity, then delivered a final, bout-ending kick.

Norris was once asked whether anyone could duplicate Bruce's technique.

"Bruce's style was pretty much Bruce's," he answered.

Return of the Dragon was released in the United States after his fourth film, *Enter the Dragon*. Bruce was thirty-two, healthy, and working hard in Hong Kong on yet another film, *Game of Death*, when tragedy struck.

According to the official story, on the afternoon of July 30, 1973, Bruce had gone to the apartment of actress Betty Ting-Pei to discuss a role for her in one of his upcoming movies. He complained of a headache and was given a painkiller called Equagesic, and then went into the bedroom to rest. When he couldn't be awakened, he was rushed to Queen Elizabeth Hospital. Doctors sought to revive him but could not. Within an hour, he was pronounced dead.

There were two funerals, one in Hong Kong where 25,000 to 30,000 people showed up. Later, there was a quieter service in Seattle. He was buried to the music of "The Impossible Dream" and "My Way."

One of the first doctor's reports linked Bruce's death to cannabis poisoning and brain swelling. [Cannabis is another term for such drugs as marijuana and hashish.] But that report only puzzled experts. Several agreed with Dr. Milton Halpern, medical examiner for the city of New York, who said he knew of no "acute case of intoxication by cannabis."

Another expert said that cannabis poisoning could occur only under the rarest of circumstances, as when an individual is able to obtain a highly concentrated form of the drug. But cannabis in this form, it was pointed out, is normally available only for research purposes.

Later, a Hong Kong coroner rejected marijuana as a cause of Bruce's death. The coroner's verdict was "death by misadventure." The technical term he used was "acute cerebral edema," or buildup of fluid in the brain.

This swelling could have been caused by reaction to Equagesic or Dolanex. This last-named was a drug Bruce had been taking for a back injury. Doctors pointed out that the swelling could also have been caused by some natural illness. Several doctors agreed that Bruce's brain was "swollen like a sponge."

Bruce's swarms of fans could not accept these explanations. The rumors continued. As his wife put it, ". . . that a man of Bruce's astonishing virility, vitality, energy, and sheer physical fitness should blank out like a snuffed candle? Perhaps people can't be blamed for speculating."

Concerning Bruce's death, there is a theory to suit every taste. Overwork was suggested as the cause. Bruce pushed himself to incredible lengths, training fanatically in his specially equipped gym, doing endless thumb pushups. Perhaps he eventually just burned himself out.

It was said he may have died from his strange diet of raw beef, eggs, and milk. Or his passing may have resulted from his special high-protein drink or his habit of drinking cow's blood.

When Bruce's coffin arrived in Seattle, it was noted that it was slightly damaged during the trip from Hong Kong. To some, this was a sign that Bruce's soul was not resting easily, that perhaps he had met with foul play in some mysterious fashion. Secret herb poisons, which doctors could never detect in one's system, were mentioned.

Greedy film producers were said to have plotted Bruce's death. During the late 1970's, those who supported such a theory plastered Hong Kong with posters that proclaimed: BRUCE LEE WAS MURDERED BY HONG KONG AND WORLD-WIDE FILM KING RUN RUN SHAW.

The posters explained in careful detail how Bruce's enormous popularity and box office appeal had cut sharply into Shaw's profits. Because of the competition from Bruce's movies, Shaw had no choice but to destroy him. He cooked up an elaborate plot that involved a contract killer who poisoned Bruce. Betty Ting-Pei, in whose apartment Bruce was stricken, was said to be part of the scheme.

Even more exotic was the belief that Bruce had died of a martial arts ritual known as "The Iron Fist" or "The Vibrating Hand." It was said that several elder martial arts masters were upset with Bruce and his films because he was giving away too many ancient martial arts secrets. The masters sent a representative to talk to Bruce, hoping to convince him to stop making films. Bruce, never a diplomat, laughed at the idea. So the masters' representative, a Great Master himself, simply laid his hand on Bruce's shoulder, applying "The Iron Fist."

Weeks later, Bruce's body functions began to slow down and his interest in martial arts and film-making started to ebb. He soon died. This is no joke. More than a few martial arts students and instructors believe Bruce to be a victim of "The Iron Fist."

What caused Bruce Lee's death? There is a

theory to suit every taste. The debate continues. The aura of mystery that surrounds Bruce Lee's passing is not going to go away.

In the years immediately following his death, Bruce's films earned tens of millions of dollars. *Enter the Dragon*, the last movie he completed before his death, became one of Warner Brothers' all-time international moneymakers. Hong Kong producers sought to cash in on his popularity with films starring an army of Bruce Lee lookalikes and soundalikes. There was Bruce Lei, Bruce Li, and Dragon Lee, to name only a few.

The films were only part of the boom. There were paperback books, albums, T-shirts, sweat-shirts, and posters, all meant to memorialize Bruce.

Early in the 1990s, Universal Pictures began developing a new film celebrating Bruce's life, called *Dragon: The Bruce Lee Story*. It was suggested that Brandon Lee, Bruce's son, who was pursuing an acting career, might be cast in the leading role. But the 25-year-old Brandon said that he didn't want to be considered. The part eventually went to Jason Scott Lee (no relation to Bruce), a 26-year-old Chinese-Hawaiian actor.

As for Brandon, he was leading a rebellious life not unlike that of his father. He had been thrown out of two high schools and had dropped out of another. Like his father, Brandon had gone to Asia to make his first feature films, then returned to the United States. In 1991, he costarred in his first Hollywood movie, *Showdown in Little Tokyo*.

Better roles started coming. In 1993, he began

work on a film that he felt would give him a chance to display his talent as a dramatic actor. Titled *The Crow*, the movie told the story of a murdered rock star who, through supernatural power, takes the form of a bird to avenge his girlfriend's death and his own.

From the beginning, the production of *The Crow* was troubled by one problem after another. A technician was severely burned. Another worker slipped and drove a screwdriver through his hand. A publicist was injured in an auto accident. The weather in Wilmington, North Carolina, where the movie was filmed, was unseasonably cold and wet and storms destroyed some of the sets. As the film neared completion, Brandon was on the brink of exhaustion.

He had only three days of filming left when a fatal accident occurred. Brandon was fatally shot by a 44-caliber bullet fired from a gun that was supposed to be loaded with blanks. In the years since, almost as many questions have been asked about Brandon's death as about his father's.

After memorial services in Los Angeles, Brandon was buried in Seattle beside his father. As a family friend remarked, father and son died "as they just were beginning."

America has a growing roster of cultural legends, men and women who, in death, loom larger than in life. Their spirit touches one generation after another. There is John Wayne, who typifies the Old West and also carries a sense of patriotism; there is James Dean, the eternal rebel; Marilyn

Monroe, the Hollywood goddess; Elvis Presley, King of Rock 'n' Roll; and John Lennon, part of a fabled musical tradition. And now there is Bruce Lee, a martial artist without equal and the ultimate man of action.

The *Hindenburg* Disaster

The giant zeppelin *Hindenburg*, the biggest airship ever built, was three city blocks long, but its final flight over New York City was so low that passengers waved from open windows to news photographers they could almost reach out and touch atop the Empire State Building. That was more than fifty years ago, on May 6, 1937.

The *Hindenburg*, "The Great Floating Palace," as it was sometimes called, made the Atlantic crossing from its home base in Frankfurt, Germany, in just over two days, half the time needed by the fastest ocean liner. It would be another twenty years before transatlantic flight by commercial airplanes would begin.

Staterooms were comfortable and quiet for the thirty-six passengers each of whom had paid a fare of $400. The normal crew of around fifty had been increased to sixty-one with the addition of eleven trainees. Fine meals were served on blue and gold porcelain. Passengers could leave their shoes outside their stateroom doors at night, and in the morning they would be polished.

Passengers traveled aboard the *Hindenburg* secure in the knowledge that no fare-paying customer had ever been killed or injured on one of Germany's airships, this despite the fact they were inflated with explosive hydrogen. The *Hindenburg* had begun commercial service the year before, in 1936, and had made ten round trips between the United States and Germany and six round trips to Rio de Janeiro.

The airship's usual flight from Frankfurt to the United States took the *Hindenburg* over the Netherlands, then the North Sea, and England as it headed for Newfoundland, the shortest transatlantic route. The captain often came close to skimming the waves so passengers could see the giant icebergs. The *Hindenburg* had the U.S. Naval Air Station at Lakehurst, New Jersey, as its destination.

On its flight of May 6, 1937, the *Hindenburg* was delayed by stiff headwinds over the Atlantic. Instead of arriving at 6 A.M., as scheduled, the landing was postponed to 6 P.M.

When the *Hindenburg* arrived over Lakehurst, Captain Max Pruss, the airship's commanding officer, didn't like the menacing look of the black clouds he saw. A cold front accompanied by a thunderstorm was approaching. Captain Pruss decided to take the airship a few miles to the south to avoid the bad weather. He returned to Lakehurst not long after 7 P.M. and made preparations to land.

The mooring party of over 200 men watched

the airship circle in the gray sky. A light rain was falling. Captain Pruss eased the huge airship toward its 160-foot mooring mast, then ordered the engines reversed. The great airship hung in the air.

Passengers crowded at the windows, hoping to catch a glimpse of relatives or friends who were waiting. Trail ropes dropped from the airship were connected to ground lines by the mooring party. Everything seemed perfectly normal.

One of those watching the dramatic scene unfold was Herbert Morrison, a radio news reporter for station WLS in Chicago. Morrison's job was to tape a description of the landing for use on the station's *Dinner Bell* program the next day.

"Passengers are looking out the windows, waving," Morrison said into his microphone, trying to make the broadcast interesting. "The ship is standing still now. The vast motors are just holding it."

"Here it comes, ladies and gentlemen, and what a sight it is, a thrilling one, a marvelous sight . . . The sun is striking the windows of the observation deck on the westward side and sparkling like glittering jewels on a background of black velvet . . ."

Suddenly, Morrison's voice became filled with anxiety and even hysteria as a plume of flame burst from the top of the airship.

"Oh, oh, oh . . . ," Morrison cried.

"It's burst into flames . . . Get out of the way, please; oh my, this is terrible. Oh my, get out of the way, please! It's burning, bursting into flames and falling . . . Oh! This is one of the worst . . . Oh! It's a terrific sight . . . Oh! And all the humanity! . . .

"I can't talk, ladies and gentlemen . . . I have to stop for a minute, for this is one of the worst things I have ever witnessed."

To Morrison and the horror-stricken spectators who watched from the ground, the first flames appeared at the rear of the airship just forward of the *Hindenburg*'s upper tail fin. Within seconds, the tail dropped and the whole length of the airship was engulfed in flame. As the giant torch went crashing to the ground tailfirst, a long jet of flame poured from the top. Then the whole front section fell to earth, crushing the passenger section.

"People were still inside; we helped them get out," a member of the ground crew recalls. "One man — all he had on was his shoes. They were still smoldering, but he was walking; then he collapsed."

A number of people managed to save themselves by jumping from the airship's windows before it hit the ground. An acrobat and dancer named Joseph Spak landed on his feet, breaking an ankle. Most jumpers, however, suffered serious injuries.

One elderly woman walked out through the airship's regular exit as if nothing were happening — and was untouched. Another passenger tore his way through a thick tangle of hot metal using his bare hands. Still another managed to get out safely, only to have another passenger land on top of him, and injure him seriously. One man, at an open window and with a chance to jump for safety, went back into the flames to search for his wife; both died.

It all happened so suddenly that it seemed as if no one could possibly have lived through the disaster. Yet sixty-two of the ninety-seven passengers and crew members managed to survive, although many were seriously burned or injured.

The fire burned for three hours, feeding on the many tons of diesel fuel that were aboard. Whiskey and wine bottles kept exploding, sounding like heavy gunfire.

When it was over, all that was left was the charred skeleton of the once great airship that was almost 804 feet in length, 103 feet in diameter. Souvenir hunters sifted through the debris. Some of them carted away scorched pieces of the *Hindenburg*'s silver-gray outer covering. Today, small squares and rectangles of this fabric are sometimes offered for sale at antique shops and flea markets.

The *Hindenburg* disaster truly marked the end of an era. What at the time had been hailed as a safe, smooth, efficient means of international transport, was abandoned overnight. A half-century passed before any other lighter-than-air craft carried a paying customer. On May 6, 1987, fifty years to the day following the *Hindenburg* tragedy, a British company began offering airship flights that circled San Francisco Bay for $150 a passenger.

The flights were part of a revival of airships that occurred during the 1980's. Several airships

— the Goodyear blimp was typical — found use as airborne platforms for television cameras and for advertising purposes. But these were nonrigid airships. They had no internal framework; they were mere airbags. The *Hindenburg* had an elaborate internal framework made of aluminum alloy.

And modern-day blimps are small by comparison. Three or four Goodyear-style airships could have been lined up end-to-end and placed inside the *Hindenburg*.

How did the *Hindenburg* disaster happen? Why did it happen? Who caused it to happen?

Almost from the day the *Hindenburg* disaster took place, investigators sought to answer these questions. As a result of the investigations, several theories were put forth. None, however, has been proven to be valid. To this day, the cause of the tragedy has not been determined with any certainty.

To understand what might have happened to the *Hindenburg*, it's necessary to be aware of the political situation that prevailed at the time. Adolph Hitler, the leader of the National Socialist Party, the Nazis, had come to power in Germany in 1933. Hitler urged the use of force to create a "Greater Germany." He drafted German men into the army, created an air force, and began to build submarines. Soon Europe would be on the brink of war.

Even the *Hindenburg* itself became a symbol of Nazism. The vertical tailfins of the airship were blazoned with the swastika, the official emblem of the Nazi party. And during the national elections in Germany in 1936, the *Hindenburg* had been fitted with loudspeakers and used to blare Nazi-party propaganda to voters.

Earlier in the 1930's, when the *Hindenburg* was in a planning stage, its designers and builders wanted to use nonflammable helium as the airship's lifting gas. Helium is extracted from natural gas, which, at the time, was found only in the United States and the Soviet Union. But the United States refused to approve selling helium to Germany, which was beginning to loom as an enemy nation.

Unable to obtain helium, the builders of the *Hindenburg* had to rely on hydrogen, one of the most explosive and hottest burning of all gases, to keep the airship aloft. In fact, the *Hindenburg* was inflated with 7,000,000 cubic feet of hydrogen which was contained in sixteen huge cloth compartments, called cells.

Because the tiniest spark could ignite the hydrogen, elaborate precautions were taken aboard the airship. Passengers had to surrender any matches or cigarette lighters they were carrying as they came aboard. Those who wanted to smoke aboard the *Hindenburg* had to enter a specially built smoking room with a double-door entrance that was meant to keep out the smallest amount of hydrogen. The room was equipped with cigarette lighters that were chained down so no one could carry one off to another, nonfireproof part of the airship.

No flashlights were allowed aboard, either. Only

safety lamps, like those worn by miners, were permitted. A six-year-old boy was made to surrender his toy automobile because, when pushed, it threw off sparks.

Members of the crew whose duties called for them to stride the spindly catwalks between the fabric cells that held the hydrogen had to be on constant guard against static electricity and the sparks that resulted from it. They wore buttonless coveralls and shoes with hemp soles.

Many investigators, both German and American, agreed the spark that had caused the hydrogen to explode had a natural source. It was an "act of God," said one expert.

For example, one investigator said that the manila ropes dropped to the ground as the Hindenburg approached its mooring mast could have created a discharge of static electricity. The resulting sparks could have then touched off any hydrogen that might have escaped from the fuel cells or leaking valves.

One witness who came before a panel of investigators testified that he saw the dim blue light of a phenomenon known as St. Elmo's fire on the top of the airship before it burst into flames. St. Elmo's fire, sometimes seen on the wings of airplanes during an electrical storm, can occur anytime the atmosphere is so highly charged with electricity that a discharge is created between an object and the air.

Most experts agreed that there were pockets of hydrogen within the airship waiting to be ignited.

According to Dr. Hugo Eckener, one of the foremost airship experts of the day, and who served as the captain of the *Hindenburg* on its early transatlantic flights, the *Hindenburg*'s last turn overstressed the hull and snapped a bracing wire. The wire's end could have sliced through the fabric of a gas cell like a razor, said Dr. Eckener. Torsion gauges salvaged from the wreckage tended to support Dr. Eckener's theory. They showed the bracing wires to be under extremely high tension as the *Hindenburg* maneuvered to land.

Another expert had a theory similar to Dr. Eckener's. He was Captain Hans von Schiller, the commanding officer of the *Graf Zeppelin*, which was about the same size as the *Hindenburg* and considered one of the most successful airships ever built. Captain von Schiller once admitted that there were always "a few leaks of hydrogen" on airships.

In attempting to explain what happened aboard the *Hindenburg*, von Schiller explained, " . . . when an airship lands, it reverses its engines, just as a ship does. And, like a ship, it vibrates. An airship could vibrate so much, it could break a bracing wire.

"These bracing wires are thick," von Schiller said, "and when they snap, heat is generated at the break. Now if the hot end of the wire recoiled into the buildup of leaking gas, this could have caused the fire."

But many investigators refused to believe that the *Hindenburg* disaster had a natural cause, that an "act of God" was responsible. They were attracted to the idea of sabotage. An enemy agent had triggered the explosion.

They reasoned that it would not have been difficult to place an incendiary device near the airship's tail, where the fire had started. There was a ladder there, which the saboteur could have used, and a ventilation shaft that would have fanned the flames.

Nazi leaders, however, would not even discuss the sabotage theory. The destruction of the *Hindenburg* had been a sharp blow to the pride of Nazi flag-wavers. For them to admit sabotage had been the cause would have been also to admit that the enemies of Nazism had scored a telling victory; it would have humiliated them.

Nevertheless, sabotage was a topic that very much concerned the German government. The backgrounds of all passengers aboard the *Hindenburg* had been carefully checked. Luggage had been opened and searched for weapons and explosive devices. While luggage inspections are common today, with international terrorism a fact of life, in the 1930's they were practically unheard of. It was also rumored that a couple of SS men, that is, members of Hitler's special police force, had been planted among the crew to keep an eye on the passengers.

Trying to find proof of sabotage was no easy matter. The *Hindenburg* had burned so completely that there were few clues remaining. Aside from the charred aluminum framework, about all investigators had to look at were small pieces of fabric, scraps of scorched letters, aluminum furniture that had melted into weird shapes. And there were ashes, bushels and bushels of ashes.

Amidst the ashes, investigators found pieces of material — zinc oxide, graphite, and manganese dioxide — that could have been used in the manufacture of a small battery, a dry cell, the kind used to power flashlights, children's toys, or small portable radios, or camera flashbulb systems.

They also found the remains of a timing device. This evidence seemed to indicate that perhaps the *Hindenburg* had been destroyed by a saboteur, after all.

Investigators, however, avoided saying that sabotage was the cause of the tragedy. Doing so would have created serious international problems, they believed. There was enough tension in the world at the time; they did not want to add to it.

If it was sabotage, who was the saboteur? At least two investigations have focused on a member of the crew, a tall, fair-haired young man named Eric Spehl. Spehl's job as a rigger would have required him to use the lofty catwalk within the airship's interior, which put him in close contact with the gas cells.

On the day the *Hindenburg* burned, Spehl had been on duty at the rear of the airship, where the fire had started, until 6 P.M. After going off duty, Spehl had gone to the forward section of the airship, and he was there when the fire erupted.

But being a good distance from the point of the explosion proved of no benefit to Spehl, for he was one of those who died.

Spehl was 23 when, in 1933, he was hired to help build the *Hindenburg*. When not working, Spehl spent his time taking photographs and working in the darkroom he had built for himself.

Some investigators believe that Spehl planted a flashbulb and timing device within one of the airship's gas cells. The tremendous heat generated by the exploding bulb ignited the hydrogen in an instant.

It's believed that Spehl didn't intend to kill anyone, and certainly not himself. The timer was set to touch off the flashbulb after the *Hindenburg* had landed and the passengers and crew members had left the airship. But something went wrong. Perhaps the timing device malfunctioned. Or maybe the headwinds and thunderstorms that delayed the airship's arrival upset Spehl's plans.

Why would young Eric Spehl have wanted to destroy the *Hindenburg*? Perhaps because he had anti-Nazi sympathies and was beginning to ally himself with the Communist Party. Germany and Japan had recently signed a pact to oppose Communism. In other words, Spehl's politics were his motivation.

No one is certain that Spehl is the guilty party. There are no witnesses to what he might have done; there is no direct evidence.

For well over half a century, people have been intrigued by the story of the *Hindenburg*. Part of that fascination stems from the mystery of how the great airship was destroyed. Was the disastrous fire that devoured the *Hindenburg* sparked by a random accident or some "act of God," or was what happened the work of a saboteur? No one can say for sure. What took place over the wet and sandy landing field at Lakehurst remains, as one expert has called it, "one of the most tragic and mysterious accidents in the prewar history of air travel."

Movie Star Mystery

On a quiet Sunday morning late in November 1981, the body of film star Natalie Wood was found floating face down just below the surface of the water in a quiet patch of the Pacific Ocean off the remote northern end of Santa Catalina Island, twenty-six miles from the coast of California. When the body was sighted, it was approximately a mile away from the *Splendour*, the quarter-million-dollar yacht owned by the star and her actor-husband Robert Wagner. Natalie's death was officially listed as "accidental drowning."

As her devastated husband, her many show business friends, and her fans around the world mourned her passing, everyone seemed to be asking: How did Natalie Wood die? What happened? While there are many theories, the questions have never been satisfactorily answered.

It was Los Angeles County Medical Examiner Thomas Noguchi who, after investigating Natalie's death, decided it should be labeled "accidental." But later Noguchi, who lost his job partly as a result of the storm of controversy that followed Natalie's death, urged that the case be reopened. But it never has been.

Beautiful and beloved, 43-year-old Natalie Wood had been one of Hollywood's biggest stars for almost three decades, although her performances didn't always please the critics. "She is brassy and mechanical," said one, "with wind-up emotions." But it was generally agreed by the public that Natalie never gave a bad performance, no matter how horrible the film.

Her movies — *Rebel Without a Cause, Kings Go Forth, Marjorie Morningstar, West Side Story, Gypsy, Love With the Proper Stranger, Splendor in the Grass, Bob & Carol, Ted & Alice* among them — had earned her enormous wealth and fame.

Natalie's life was the often-told Hollywood tale of the bright-eyed child who becomes a screen legend. She was born Natasha Gurdin of Russian immigrant parents in San Francisco on July 20, 1938. The family was poor but Natasha's mother realized that her radiant young daughter could be the breadwinner. At five, she was cast in *Tomorrow Is Forever*, a film in which she managed to steal several scenes from veteran actor Orson Welles. "She was so good," Welles once recalled, "she frightened me."

By the time Natalie was eight, she was on her way to becoming a household name, thanks to a warm and tender performance as a little girl who didn't believe in Santa Claus in *Miracle on 34th Street*. The film is a classic, rerun on television more often than the *Wizard of Oz*. Less than two years after the movie's debut, Natalie was earning more than a thousand dollars a week.

Natalie made her mark as a teenage star playing opposite James Dean in *Rebel Without a Cause*, another film that became a classic. By the time Natalie was ready to graduate from Van Nuys High School, she was socializing with two of the cast members, Nick Adams and Sal Mineo. They, along with Dean, made up the Hollywood Brat Pack of their generation.

All three suffered early and tragic deaths. Dean was killed in an auto accident before *Rebel* was released. Adams died under mysterious circumstances, a possible suicide, and Mineo was stabbed to death during a robbery attempt.

After James Dean's death, Natalie dated a succession of Hollywood bachelors, including Elvis Presley. The two young superstars went everywhere together. Often they were spotted racing around town on Elvis's motorcycle or cruising about in his white Cadillac convertible.

Natalie was eighteen and Robert Wagner twenty-six when the two began dating. Known as R.J. to his friends, Wagner was Hollywood's most glamorous bachelor, the object of affection for countless teenage movie fans. Natalie and R.J. were married in 1957 but they divorced four years later. "We loved each other tremendously," Natalie was later to say. "It was disillusioning when it didn't work out. It made me feel that it's not an easy thing, marriage, not easy at all."

Natalie tried marriage a second time in 1968 with British agent-producer Richard Gregson. Gregson, at thirty-eight, was nine years older than Natalie. The couple had a daughter, Natasha, born in 1970. They were divorced in 1971.

Not long after, Natalie and Bob Wagner rediscovered one another. On July 16, 1972, aboard a yacht with only family and friends on hand, R.J. and Natalie were remarried. She gave birth to her second daughter, Courtney Brooke Wagner, on March 9, 1974.

In the years between their divorce and remarriage, the professional status of R.J. and Natalie had changed. He was now enjoying greater success than she was, largely because of *Hart to Hart*, the successful TV series in which he starred. Natalie was not quite as popular as she once had been.

Although her career may have been past its peak, Natalie seemed secure. Her marriage was thought to be solid, one of the best in Hollywood, in fact. She was a devoted and loving mother to Natasha and Courtney and to R.J.'s daughter Kate.

Eager to keep busy as an actress, Natalie accepted a leading role in *Brainstorm*, a science-fiction film about a machine that was able to transfer one person's thoughts and emotions to another. Natalie's co-star was to be Christopher Walken, a rising thirty-eight-year-old actor. Walken's performance in *The Deer Hunter* in 1978 had won him an Oscar as Best Supporting Actor.

After several weeks of work on *Brainstorm* in North Carolina, the cast was given some time off.

Thursday, November 26, was Thanksgiving Day, and the Wagners took advantage of the break in filming to invite several relatives and a few friends to their home for dinner. Her sister, Lana, recalled that Natalie seemed "incredibly tense" that day. She described her as " . . . a very different Natalie from the one I had last seen before she began shooting *Brainstorm*."

During the afternoon, Natalie disclosed to her guests that she and R.J. were planning to go out on the *Splendour* for a few days. "Chris Walken is coming with us," she said. "The weather should be perfect." Then Natalie spoke individually to several of her friends, inviting them to join them aboard the *Splendour* for the weekend. But each declined, saying the pressure of work was too great.

The *Splendour* arrived off Catalina on the Friday after Thanksgiving. Natalie, R.J., and Walken spent the afternoon shopping and sightseeing in Avalon, a small community on the island's southern tip.

That night, Natalie, R.J., and Walken were joined by Dennis Davern, the *Splendour*'s skipper, and the four had dinner ashore at Doug's Harbor Reef restaurant. They returned to spend the night aboard the yacht.

By coincidence, Paul Miller, an adviser to the Los Angeles Medical Examiner's Officer, and a friend of Wagner's, was also dining at Doug's Harbor Reef restaurant that evening. Miller and his friends couldn't help but notice Natalie, her husband, and their guests happily drinking champagne at another table.

The Wagners were still enjoying themselves when Miller and his friends left the restaurant to return to their boat. A cold rainstorm had swept in off the ocean but the sea was not rough.

Later that night aboard his boat, Miller and his wife could not sleep because of loud music coming from a party on shore. Around 1:15 A.M., Miller picked up his radio microphone to call the Coast Guard to ask them to quiet the party. Just as he did, a message blared from the radio's speaker. It was Bob Wagner's voice. "This is the *Splendour*," Wagner said. "We think we may have someone missing in an eleven-foot rubber dinghy."

Before long, Harbor Patrol boats, private boats, and Coast Guard helicopters had taken up the search. At 7:30 that morning, a crew member aboard one of the helicopters spotted a blotch of red in the water below. It was Natalie's body. She was wearing a red down-filled jacket.

The body was recovered about a mile from the *Splendour*. Shortly after, the missing dinghy was discovered on a beach a little bit farther to the south. Oddly, the boat's ignition switch was in the "off" position and the oars were still tied down. Investigators were surprised that the boat obviously had not been used.

Even more bizarre was the fact that Natalie was wearing only a nightgown, knee-length wool socks, and the red down jacket. It was obvious that Natalie had not dressed for an early morning boat trip into town. Yet police theorized that she must have been the one who untied the line that secured the dinghy to the yacht.

But why had she untied the boat if she didn't intend to go out in it? That was just one of the many questions surrounding the mystery that lacked an answer.

Later that day, Wagner made a statement to police that covered his version of events. He said that after returning to the yacht, he and Walken had gone into the boat's main cabin for a nightcap. Natalie retired to their cabin. That was about 10:45 P.M. It was the last time he remembered seeing his wife.

Sometime after midnight, Wagner went to the couple's cabin and saw his wife was not in bed. When he, Walken, and Davern searched the boat, they found that Natalie was missing and so was the dinghy. That didn't bother R.J. — at first. Natalie often took the boat out by herself. But as time passed and Natalie didn't return, Wagner began to get worried. He finally radioed for help.

The autopsy conducted by Dr. Noguchi and the Los Angeles Medical Examiner's Office found bruises on Natalie's arms and a small abrasion on her neck. An examination of her clothing revealed the nightgown, wool socks, and red down jacket were still wet after twenty-four hours. The sodden jacket was very heavy, weighing between thirty and forty pounds.

Natalie's fate may have been sealed by the weight

of the jacket that she was wearing, which pulled her below the surface when she tried to climb into the dinghy. "If she had just removed the jacket," Noguchi said, "she might have easily made it into the dinghy and survived."

Why didn't Natalie slip off the jacket? Noguchi said she might not have been thinking clearly. His laboratory report revealed that the alcohol content of Natalie's blood was .14 per cent. That's .04 per cent above the intoxication level set by the California Vehicular Department.

Noguchi called the alcohol content of Natalie's blood "a deadly factor." But Noguchi later explained, "The level of alcohol in her blood means she was only 'slightly intoxicated.'"

Noguchi's report raised almost as many questions as it answered. Some investigators, including Noguchi himself, couldn't understand why Natalie, after falling off the boat's swim step, simply didn't swim back to the step and reboard the boat. The effort would have required only a few strokes. "Even with the heavy jacket," said Noguchi, "it seemed to me she could have accomplished this effort easily."

And there was another question that Noguchi and everyone else connected with the case wanted answered: "Why had Natalie wanted to leave the *Splendour* in the middle of the night?"

Noguchi was later told by one of his staff members that Wagner and Walken had quarreled in the main cabin that night. If that was true, Noguchi believes that Natalie may have become so disgusted with the pair that she sought to take off in the dinghy.

The next day at a tense press conference, reporters wanted to know why Natalie wanted to leave the yacht. One reporter asked Noguchi, "Doctor, was there a dispute between Wagner and Walken that caused Natalie Wood to leave?"

By this time, the room was abuzz. Any argument, heated or not, could be taken to mean that Natalie's husband had contributed indirectly to her death. As the reporters continued to hammer away, Noguchi became uncomfortable. He realized that even if an argument had caused Natalie to leave the yacht, it was a secondary factor. The reason for her death was that she slipped, fell into the water, and drowned — and that's what was important.

Nevertheless, the story of Natalie's death was told beneath the screaming headlines that read: CHAMPAGNE, THEN DEATH.

In pursuit of the story, reporters went to Wagner. In seclusion, mourning Natalie's death, he had nothing to say. But some of R.J.'s friends sought to quiet the rumors by telling reporters that there had been no argument between Wagner and Walken. Instead, they explained, Natalie had been unable to sleep because the dinghy, tied to the yacht's stern, was bumping against the side of the boat. Because the thumping was keeping her awake, Natalie left the cabin and went up onto the deck to tighten the line securing the dinghy. While attempting to do so, she slipped and fell into the water.

To Noguchi, that sounded reasonable. And it would help to explain why Natalie was dressed in socks and a down jacket.

Paul Miller, whom Wagner had radioed first the night of the accident, was one person who didn't believe Noguchi's explanation that Natalie had fallen into the water and drowned next to the yacht. He had another theory. Miller concluded that the dinghy was found on a beach more than a mile from the *Splendour* because Natalie had taken it there.

According to Miller's theory, Natalie was attempting to get aboard the dinghy when she fell. Once in the water, just a few feet from the yacht, Natalie hooked her right arm over the side of the dinghy, knowing that it would keep her afloat while she caught her breath and figured out what to do next. (A bruise on her right arm tended to confirm this, Miller said.) But as she clung to the dinghy, she and the boat were swept to the south by the wind. Within a matter of seconds, she was too far away from the *Splendour* to attempt to swim back.

Undoubtedly Natalie called out for help at this point. But her cries went unanswered. They were probably drowned out by blaring party music from other boats. Wagner, Walken, and Davern said they were below deck on the *Splendour* and never heard anything.

Marilyn Wayne, a guest on a yacht that happened to be moored about 200 yards away from the *Splendour*, said she thought she heard screams coming from Wagner's yacht the night Natalie drowned. Wayne told investigators, according to a story in the *Los Angeles Times*, "My friend woke me up in the boat around 11:45 and said, 'Do you hear a woman calling for help?' I listened through the porthole and I could hear someone saying, 'Help me, somebody. Please help me!' " But when Wayne looked out the porthole, she could see no one.

As the wind continued to push the dinghy away from the yacht, Natalie struggled to climb into it. But she could not. The bulky, cylinder-shaped sides of the dinghy prevented her from getting a solid grip and hoisting herself up out of the water. And the water-soaked down jacket kept pulling her back down. Fingernail scratches on the side of the rubber craft were evidence of her struggle.

When Natalie found she was unable to climb into the dinghy, Paul Miller believes she probably tried to propel the rubber boat toward the Catalina shore. She kicked with her legs and paddled with her free arm.

Slowly, the dinghy started heading toward the shoreline. But Natalie couldn't keep up the fight. Her arms and legs grew weary. Numbness from the cold water wracked her entire body. She stopped paddling with her arm; she stopped kicking with her legs. Finally, she no longer had even the strength to keep gripping the side of the boat and she slipped below the surface. Minutes later, the boat touched onto the sandy beach.

The controversy over what actually may have

happened aboard the *Splendour* that last fateful weekend of Natalie's life continued for years. It was fueled at least in part by stories of heated arguments involving Natalie, R.J., Walken, and Davern, on and off the boat.

Natalie's relatives and friends have tried to shrug off the stories. "The only important thing," said Paul Ziffren, her lawyer, "is that Natalie is gone. The rest is ghoulish nonsense."

Sometime after the tragedy, Wagner tried to sell the *Splendour*. But he could find no buyer. People said the *Splendour* was cursed. Wagner ended up donating the yacht to a charitable institution. After renaming it *The Graceful Lady*, the charity managed to sell the craft.

To this day, Natalie Wood's lonely death still puzzles people. And no wonder. When a beautiful movie star stumbles off a quarter-million-dollar yacht in her nightgown in the middle of the night, and there is not a single witness to explain what really happened, it's bound to raise some questions.

A President's
Mysterious Death

Abraham Lincoln. James A. Garfield. William McKinley. John F. Kennedy. To this list of murdered American presidents, some historians would willingly add the name of Warren G. Harding.

But unlike Lincoln, Garfield, McKinley, and Kennedy, who were gunned down in public by social misfits, Harding, the nation's twenty-ninth president, died a quiet death, while resting comfortably in a San Francisco hotel suite.

With him at the time was his wife, Florence Kling Harding, a drab, unsmiling, high-strung, strong-willed woman. Mrs. Harding always had the highest hopes for her husband. She helped to persuade him to run for the U.S. Senate and later the presidency. But more than a few sources suggest this powerful woman was also the cause of her husband's death.

Mrs. Harding certainly had reasons for ending her husband's life, at least in her own mind. A great tide of graft and corruption was threatening to engulf the Harding administration. In the months to come, Mrs. Harding foresaw humiliation and disgrace, and perhaps even impeachment and imprisonment. Her husband's death would serve to preserve his reputation, she may have thought. No one would think of denouncing a deceased president. Her husband might even come to be looked upon as a martyr.

The belief that foul play was the cause of President Harding's death was strengthened when Mrs. Harding refused to allow an autopsy. And in the months following the President's passing, Mrs. Harding gathered up and destroyed her husband's official papers. Little wonder that she is looked upon with suspicion.

Several years after the President's death, a book appeared by Gaston Means, who had worked as an investigator in the Justice Department during Harding's administration. Titled *The Strange Death of President Harding*, the book claimed what many people had been whispering: that Florence Harding had poisoned her husband.

The final scene in the President's bedroom was one of great confusion. Several different accounts of what happened in the moments before his passing appeared in the press. Not until two days after he had died was an official version of events made public.

Mrs. Harding died fifteen months after her husband. It's likely the real story of what happened went with her to the grave.

Warren G. Harding was born on November 2, 1865, on a farm near Corsica (now Blooming Grove), Ohio, the oldest of eight children. After attending local public schools, Harding went to Ohio Central College in Iberia.

Afterward, Harding tried teaching, then sold insurance for a while, and thought about becoming a lawyer. He didn't find a profession he really liked until he tried newspaper work, joining the staff of the Marion *Democratic Mirror*.

In 1884, when Harding was nineteen, he and two friends borrowed the $300 needed to buy a newspaper, the Marion (Ohio) *Star*, which was deeply in debt at the time. But with Harding as editor, and business manager and typesetter as well, the paper became more lively and eventually began to prosper.

As the editor of a thriving newspaper, Harding got to know local community leaders and political bosses. Tall and good-looking, with a quick smile and an easygoing manner, he played in the town band and frequently attended local sporting events.

In 1891, Harding married Florence Kling DeWolfe, the daughter of a Marion banker. With the marriage, Harding's life began to change. Mrs. Harding, whom he nicknamed the "Duchess," a dominating woman, pulled the strings that helped to make her husband an important figure in the community. Harding became a member of Marion's leading civic organizations and the director of several successful corporations.

At his wife's urging, Harding decided to embark upon a political career. He made rapid progress. He was elected to the state senate in 1900 and became lieutenant governor in 1903, but lost in an election for governor in 1910.

During this time, Harding came under the influence of Harry M. Daugherty, a lobbyist and political strategist. Daugherty and Mrs. Harding worked as a team to boost Harding's political career. In 1914, with Daugherty as his campaign manager, Harding ran successfully for a seat in the U.S. Senate.

Harding thoroughly enjoyed being a senator. He liked the clublike atmosphere of the Senate itself and the prestige that went with the job. While he opposed high taxes and the federal regulation of business, Harding made no memorable speeches in the Senate nor did he sponsor any important legislation. He spent a good deal of his time seeking government jobs for his friends.

Early in 1920, when the Republicans began to seek a presidential candidate, Harding's name was sometimes mentioned. Harding shrugged off such recognition. All he wanted to do was remain in the Senate, where he was enjoying himself. But his ambitious wife convinced him he should have higher goals.

Most of the delegates to the Republican convention in Chicago that summer supported candidates other than Harding. But Daugherty, aided by Mrs. Harding, was busy behind the scenes. When the convention became deadlocked, Daugherty, other political leaders, and a small group of senators met in a room at the Blackstone Hotel and decided that Harding should be the Republican Party's presidential nominee. Shortly after, the convention confirmed their choice. In the presidential election that November, Harding easily defeated James Cox, the Democrats' candidate.

At first, all went well for the new president. He cut taxes and removed controls that had been in effect since World War I, which had ended in 1918. "Back to Normalcy," had been Harding's campaign slogan, and that was the course he set to pursue as president.

Mrs. Harding had other aims. She took a greater interest in her husband's foreign policy than in domestic affairs or the business of government. She looked forward to the day when she and her husband would make a grand triumphant tour of Europe, calling upon the kings and rulers of the world. "This is the age of woman," she declared. "For the first time in American history, a woman shall be recorded as a real factor, a power, and not have to go by that uninteresting and moth-eaten title: First Lady of the Land. Silly!"

But Mrs. Harding's grand plans were threatened by tales of corruption that began to filter out of the White House. Harding had brought many of his friends to Washington and placed them in powerful jobs. They became known as the "Ohio

Gang." After some of them betrayed the President in their quest for money and position, fear and suspicion spread like an epidemic.

When Harding had arrived in Washington, one of his first moves had been to appoint Harry M. Daugherty to be his attorney general. Daugherty's office teemed with corruption. He was later tried, but two juries were unable to agree upon a verdict, and Daugherty was released.

The Daugherty problem wasn't the worst of it. Harding was also shaken when Jesse W. Smith, a close friend of Daugherty's, committed suicide in May 1923. It had been revealed that Smith was guilty of handling Department of Justice money. Similar wrongdoings led to the suicide of Charles F. Cramer, legal adviser to the Veterans' Bureau, and to the jailing of Charles R. Forbes, the director of the agency.

"Teapot Dome" was the name given to the most serious of the scandals. It was one of the worst in U.S. history, in fact. It involved leases on oil-rich property owned by the U.S. Navy in Elk Hills, California, and Teapot Dome, Wyoming.

When the U.S. Senate and a special commission began an investigation, they found that Secretary of the Interior Albert Fall had leased land to a pair of private oil companies without any competitive bidding. In return, the oil companies had "loaned" Fall $100,000. To most people, the loan looked like an outright bribe. Fall resigned from his post in 1923. He was later sentenced to a year in prison in what was the first instance of a Cabinet member going to jail for crimes committed while in office.

By the summer of 1923, Harding was worried and weary. Mrs. Harding was fearful. Her husband had lost his warm, friendly, confident manner. He was looking more and more "like a hunted animal," Mrs. Harding told a friend, "with his back against the wall." Mrs. Harding was beginning to feel as if disaster was just around the corner.

In his book, *The Strange Death of President Harding*, Gaston Means gave an account of a conversation between the Hardings in which they discussed their grim future:

"Warren, I can feel it coming," said Mrs. Harding.

"What?"

"Complete exposure."

The President seemed to go to pieces, said Means. He said, "Let it come! Let it come! God, I'll be glad to have it come and get it over with!"

"You will be impeached," said Mrs. Harding.

"I will tell the truth."

"You will be disgraced."

"I will tell the truth."

"You may be imprisoned."

"I will tell the truth, the exact truth. There can be no jury of twelve American men and women who would send me to jail. But even a jail, a prison, would be peace compared to this. I am not a criminal. Let them impeach me. God knows, I'm sick and tired of it all. I'll be glad to have it over."

Mrs. Harding stared at her husband and gasped, "Are you crazy?"

"No, I am not crazy. But that, too, would be a relief, to go crazy."

Mrs. Harding had never seen her husband in such a state of mind, Means said.

The Hardings later agreed that an extended speaking tour might be a good way to revive the President's sagging spirits and restore confidence in his administration. A two-month trip, to be called a "Voyage of Understanding," was planned. It would cover a large portion of the United States and include visits to Canada and the Territory of Alaska. Neither Canada nor Alaska had ever been visited by an American president.

On June 20, 1923, the President, his wife, and some sixty-three officials, aides, and reporters boarded the train that would take them across the continent. Harding stood on the rear platform of his private car, "The Superb," and smiled and waved at the crowd as the train pulled out of Union Station.

In speeches in St. Louis, Denver, Salt Lake City, Portland, and Spokane, Harding supported the Prohibition Amendment to the Constitution, passed in 1920, which banned the manufacture and sale of alcoholic beverages. He also called for a greater stress on conservation and a tightening of immigration laws.

When the presidential party reached Tacoma, Washington, the Hardings were joined by Herbert

Hoover, the Secretary of Commerce, and his wife. Harding was very happy to see Hoover. He and his wife were excellent bridge players. Bridge was a favorite pastime of the Hardings and they and the Hoovers often played the game far into the night.

After boarding the U.S.S. *Henderson*, a Navy transport, the presidential party sailed for Metlakahla, Alaska, where they arrived on July 8. While there, Harding received a message in code from Washington about the Senate investigation into oil leases. The message had a stunning effect upon him. For the rest of the day, he seemed weary and dazed. He asked newspapermen who were accompanying the party what a president should do when his friends betrayed his trust.

After the *Henderson* left Alaska for the trip home, Harding spent much of his time working on speeches he planned to deliver on the Pacific Coast. On July 26, the presidential party arrived in Vancouver, British Columbia, where Harding gave a "good neighbor" address to a gathering of Canadians.

The following day in Seattle, Harding forecast that Alaska would one day become a state and declared that the territory must be saved from those who wanted to exploit it. The day was very hot and the sun blazed down. Several times, the President stumbled over words and toward the end of the address he appeared weak and hesitant. It was President Harding's last public appearance.

The next day, Brigadier General Charles E. Sawyer, the President's personal physician, and Lieutenant Commander Joel T. Boone, Sawyer's assistant, announced that the President had a case of indigestion and food poisoning. The condition was not serious, they agreed. All the President needed was a short rest.

The President's speeches were cancelled and he remained in bed aboard his special train as it headed south for San Francisco. A trip to Yosemite National Park was also cancelled.

On July 29, the Harding train arrived in San Francisco. The President was whisked to a suite of rooms in the Palace Hotel. General Sawyer reported the President's condition had worsened. He was suffering from stomach cramps and diarrhea and had become feverish.

The President's condition became even more serious the following day. According to General Sawyer, Harding had developed pneumonia. And now the pneumonia and food poisoning were said to be putting a strain on the President's heart.

During the next two days, the President seemed to improve. Apparently, the crisis had passed. Harding's doctors noted, however, that the President had suffered some stomach problems after eating two soft-boiled eggs.

The news was favorable again early on August 2, and the President seemed to be on the road to recovery. That evening, the nation was shocked when the news came that the President had died suddenly. "A stroke of apoplexy" was given as the cause of his death. Newspapers called it a "death stroke."

According to the official version of the events that surrounded the President's death, Mrs. Harding, who had scarcely left the President's room since they had arrived at the hotel, and General Sawyer were alone with him. Mrs. Harding was reading to her husband from an article in *The Saturday Evening Post*. Titled, "A Calm View of a Calm Man," the article praised the President for his ability to maintain his poise amidst the chaos that had beset his administration.

General Sawyer was sitting at the President's bedside, holding his hand, not for the purpose of taking his pulse or any other professional reason, but simply out of his affection for him. "It is a way with those he likes," noted *The New York Times*.

The President was propped up in bed, obviously enjoying the article that his wife was reading. "That's good. Good. Read some more," he said.

These were his last words. Suddenly, the President's body shook violently and then became still. Almost instantly, General Sawyer, still holding the President's hand, cried out, "The President is dead!"

"Do something for him!" Mrs. Harding screamed. "Give him something!"

General Sawyer grabbed a syringe from a nearby table that he had available for just such an emergency and injected a stimulant into the President's bloodstream. But nothing could be done to revive him.

After the President's death, a funeral train carried the President's body back to Washington, D.C. At places where he had been cheered by huge crowds just weeks before, people now stood silently.

The President's body lay in the East Room of the White House for a day and was then removed to the Capitol Rotunda for public viewing and the funeral. On August 10, 1923, the body was returned by train to Marion, Ohio, where it was placed in the family burial vault.

The nation was stunned by President Harding's sudden death. Reports from his doctors following his attack of indigestion from food poisoning had been generally optimistic. People were wholly unprepared for his death.

Almost immediately following the President's burial, questions began to be asked about the circumstances of his death. These served to deepen the mystery. For example, when the President first became ill, General Sawyer said that he was suffering from acute indigestion caused by eating crabmeat. But upon investigation, it was learned that the President hadn't consumed any crabmeat; there was none on the presidential menu. Further, no one who had eaten with the President before his attack of indigestion had suffered as the President had.

Many of Mrs. Harding's actions after her husband's death also caused controversy. An autopsy, an inspection of the President's body, was suggested as a means of determining the cause of the President's death. But Mrs. Harding would not permit an autopsy. Mrs. Harding also destroyed most of her husband's official papers.

There was another curious matter. It was the custom in those times to permit a sculptor to make a death mask of the deceased, so his features might be preserved. But his wife would not permit a death mask to be made of President Harding.

About a year after President Harding's death, General Sawyer died under circumstances similar to those that had claimed the life of the President. General Sawyer had just returned to his home, White Oaks Farm on the outskirts of Marion, Ohio, from his office at the Harding Memorial Association. He complained to his son, Dr. Carl W. Sawyer, that he was not feeling well. After taking some medicine, General Sawyer lay down on a couch and dropped off to sleep — and never awakened.

Mrs. Harding was living at White Oaks Farm when General Sawyer died. There were rumors that General Sawyer died because "he knew too much" and "he had to be shut up."

Several weeks after General Sawyer's passing, Mrs. Harding died, a victim of kidney disease and heart failure. *The New York Times* noted that of the nationally prominent men and women who had made the "Voyage of Understanding" to Alaska the year before, Mrs. Harding was the fifth to die. (Besides the President and General Sawyer, the others were Henry C. Wallace, Secretary of Agriculture, and Mrs. Hugo Work, wife of the Secretary of the Interior.) Mrs. Harding was said to be deeply depressed by the deaths of so many of her friends.

Evidence that Mrs. Harding may have poisoned her husband out of fear of what the Congressional investigation might reveal was offered by Gaston Means in his book, *The Strange Death of President Harding*, published in 1930. A former investigator for the Department of Justice, who often carried out special investigative assignments for Mr. Harding, and a member of the Ohio Gang, Means pulled no punches in naming Mrs. Harding as a guilty party.

In the book, Means revealed the President's final moments, as described by Mrs. Harding. Her account is somewhat different from the official version of events released at the time of Harding's death:

"I was alone with the President . . . only about ten minutes," Mrs. Harding began. "It was time for his medicine. I gave it to him; he drank it.

"He lay back on the pillow. His eyes were closed. He was resting. Then suddenly he opened his eyes wide and looked straight into my face."

"Do you think he knew?" Means asked.

"Yes, I think he knew," Mrs. Harding replied. "Then he sighed and turned his head away — over — on the pillow.

"After a few minutes, I called for help. The papers told the rest."

Whether this account of his final moments is

true or not, many of the circumstances that sur-round the death of President Harding remain to be explained. What was the actual cause of his death? Food poisoning? Pneumonia? A stroke? A heart attack? How did Mrs. Harding contribute to her husband's death? How was General Sawyer involved? These and other questions are waiting for answers.

Vanished!

Every day of the year, hundreds of people are reported missing to local police or federal law enforcement officials. Most are young runaways who return home on their own within a few days. These cases solve themselves.

But there are others, many thousands, who vanish under mysterious circumstances and never return. Some of them are individuals who carefully plan their departure, slipping away to avoid family problems or business pressures. Others who are declared missing are those men, women, or children who have been seized against their will and held for profit; they're kidnap victims. Still others are suffering from amnesia, having experienced a whole or partial loss of memory.

One of the most puzzling vanishing acts in recent years concerns Helen Vorhees Brach, the 65-year-old widow of one of the founders of the candy company known as E.J. Brach and Sons, and the heir to a sizeable fortune in property and securities. Although rewards amounting to more than

$200,000 have been offered for information leading to her whereabouts, nothing has been heard from her since the day she disappeared.

The last thing known for certain about Helen Brach is that she checked out of the Mayo Clinic in Rochester, Minnesota, on February 17, 1977. The final medical report she received showed her to be in excellent health, although one of the doctors suggested that she exercise more and lose a little weight. She paid her bill with a check.

After Mrs. Brach left the clinic, she returned to the Kahler Hotel across the street, where she had been staying, using the underground arcade that connected the two. On her way to the hotel, she stopped at a shop in the arcade to buy some bath towels and a matching soap dish and powder box, charging the purchases to her American Express account. She instructed the sales clerk to send the purchases to her new home in Florida.

Helen Brach lived in Glenview, Illinois, a residential community just north of Chicago. It had been a bitterly cold winter in the Midwest. Temperatures had plummeted to below zero half a dozen times and there had been ferocious blizzards with heavy snow. Mrs. Brach was purchasing a $200,000 apartment in Fort Lauderdale, Florida, and may have been planning to move there permanently. She had called friends in Fort Lauderdale and said she would be arriving soon, but she didn't say exactly when.

On the day she left the Mayo Clinic, Mrs. Brach had a ticket on a 2:00 P.M. flight to Chicago on

Northwest Orient Airlines. A Rochester cab driver would later recall taking Mrs. Brach to the local airport that afternoon and Northwest Orient Airlines would verify the ticket was used. However, none of the flight attendants or other members of the flight crew can recall seeing her on the plane.

Jack Matlick, the 52-year-old caretaker of Mrs. Brach's sprawling estate in Glenview, claims that "Mrs. B." or "the Missus," as he called her, arrived home on schedule. But there are no other witnesses to her arrival. Matlick says that when he met her at Chicago's O'Hare International Airport he was driving a four-wheel-drive Jeep. Mrs. Brach complained to Matlick about having to ride in such a vehicle. (Mrs. Brach collected big fancy cars. She owned a pink Lincoln Continental, a dark lavender Rolls Royce convertible, a coral-colored Cadillac sedan, and two Cadillac convertibles, one bright red, the other pink.) Matlick explained he hadn't left himself enough time to switch to one of the other cars.

Over the next few days, a number of people called the Brach home. One of the race horses that Mrs. Brach owned had won at a track in Florida, and several of her friends telephoned to congratulate her. None got to speak to Mrs. Brach, however. They were told by Matlick that she had just stepped out or was unable to come to the phone. Other callers that weekend were given similar excuses. Still others said their calls went unanswered.

One of the callers was Richard Bailey, who

owned Bailey's Stables in the Chicago suburb of Morton Grove, and who had arranged the purchases of the race horses that Mrs. Brach owned. Bailey sometimes dated Mrs. Brach. Matlick took the call and told Bailey he was surprised to hear from him because he thought he and Mrs. Brach were out on a date together. Matlick explained that someone had picked up Mrs. Brach earlier in the day, and he thought it had been Bailey.

Several outgoing calls were made from the Brach home that weekend, but none by Mrs. Brach. All were apparently placed by Matlick. One was to a decorating service. Matlick arranged for two bedrooms to be repainted and some carpeting replaced. Matlick also called a department store to order a large meat grinder.

Police who investigated Mrs. Brach's disappearance later learned that on Sunday, February 20, three days after she had checked out of the Mayo Clinic, Mrs. Brach signed a number of checks, almost all of which benefited Matlick. They included a check for $1,000, Matlick's monthly salary, and another for $3,000, which the caretaker said was a belated Christmas bonus. Matlick also received a $2,944.29 check from Mrs. Brach to pay an auto loan and a $5,500 check to buy a Cadillac, a car that had once been owned by Matlick, and which he had sold.

In addition, Matlick received a check in the amount of $1,000.40 to reimburse him for household expenses he had paid out of his own pocket. Matlick also cashed a check for $700, but he said that he was going to give the proceeds to Mrs. Brach, who planned to use the funds as pocket money on the trip she was planning to Florida.

The checks represented an unusual display of generosity by Mrs. Brach. At Christmastime, her employees normally received bonuses of less than $50.

The signatures on the checks also raised some eyebrows. They didn't look like Mrs. Brach's. Matlick explained that a trunk lid had fallen on Mrs. Brach's right wrist while she was packing for her Florida trip and it was painful for her to write, which accounted for the distorted signature.

According to Matlick, he drove Mrs. Brach to O'Hare International Airport on Monday, February 21, where she was to board a flight to Fort Lauderdale, Florida. That was four days after she had left the Mayo Clinic and Rochester, Minnesota. It was also four days after anyone remembers seeing her, except, of course, Matlick.

Matlick later told investigators that on the day of her departure for Florida Mrs. Brach was wearing a black suit, a white blouse with a black bow at the neck, and black patent leather shoes.

Helen Brach was born in Unionport, Ohio, in 1911 to Daisy and Walter Vorhees. A boy, Charles, was born to the couple seven years later.

As a teenager at Hopewell High School, Helen was tall and attractive, with reddish-gold hair. Not long after graduation, she married a local boy, but the marriage didn't last. She was divorced by the time she was twenty-one.

Helen got a job as a ticket seller for a local bus company and later worked at a pottery factory. There she eventually became a clerk in the billing department. "She had such beautiful hair," one of her coworkers once recalled. "It was red gold, and she always wore it in a long braid wound around the top of her head."

When she was thirty-two, Helen quit the pottery factory to take a job selling dance tickets at the Starlight Ballroom at Buckeye Lake, Ohio, a resort community not far from Columbus. While she was working there, she heard about a job checking coats and hats at the Indian Creek Country Club in Miami Beach, Florida, and she left Ohio to take it.

Helen was working at the country club one evening in 1950 when sixty-one-year-old Frank V. Brach, the president of E.J. Brach & Sons, a leading candy manufacturer, came into the club with his wife. The couple got into a loud argument and left together. Later, Frank Brach returned to the club alone and struck up a conversation with Helen. The two started dating and the following year, Helen, at the age of 40, became Brach's third wife.

After Brach's death in 1970, Helen continued to live in the stately eighteen-room house set on seven acres of land just off Wagner Road in Glenview, Illinois. Only Jack Matlick, the estate's caretaker, saw her on a regular basis. Matlick lived with his wife and daughters on a farm in the nearby community of Schaumberg. The farm had once been owned by the Brachs and was provided to Matlick on a rent-free basis.

Helen Brach rarely left the huge house on Wagner Road. Her nearest neighbors seldom even saw her. Quiet and conservative, she was devoted to animal causes and pet welfare projects and lavished her affection on her three dogs, Luvey, Tinkerbelle, and Beauty, but it was Matlick who fed and exercised them.

Besides her pets, Helen Brach was interested in "automatic writing." She would rise before dawn, sit down at a desk with a pencil in hand and a sheet of paper before her. She would then ask questions of the spirit world and wait for her hand to be moved across the paper in such a way as to write out the answers. Mrs. Brach kept the pages of automatic writings in a dresser drawer in her bedroom.

While Helen Brach kept her neighbors at arm's length, Jack Matlick was often rude toward them in his efforts to maintain his employer's privacy. The pair had few friends in the neighborhood. "They had this aura of money and importance about them, and they believed they had this little kingdom," John L. Demand, a former Glenview police detective, once told the *Chicago Tribune*. "Mrs. Brach seemed to look at herself as a queen. He [Matlick] thought he was the queen's general manager."

According to Matlick, when he drove Mrs. Brach to O'Hare International Airport for her flight to

Fort Lauderdale, she carried only an overnight bag. This was unusual for she often traveled with as many as forty pieces of luggage. Before she left, she told Matlick she would call him within ten days with instructions for sending her clothing and other things she had packed.

When he returned to the Brach home after dropping off Mrs. Brach, Matlick collected some of her jewelry and deposited it in a lock box at Glenview State Bank. He then took the coral-colored Cadillac to a local Cadillac agency to have it waxed and the upholstery shampooed. Later, when police questioned the workers who had done the job, they said there was nothing unusual about the condition of the car.

The decorators on Tuesday arrived to paint the two bedrooms and clean the carpeting. They, too, said there was nothing out of the ordinary about the work they were asked to do.

In the days that followed, Matlick spent most of his time at the house. Two weeks passed before he stopped in at Glenview's police headquarters to explain to police chief William Bartlett that he worked for Helen Brach and he had not heard from her since he left her at the airport. Matlick said he feared she had never arrived in Florida and he asked to fill out a missing-person report.

The police told Matlick that such a report could be filed only by the next-of-kin of the missing person. That afternoon, Matlick got in touch with Charles Vorhees, Helen's younger brother. He and his wife lived in Hopewell, Ohio. A quiet man,

Charles had recently retired from his job as an inspector of railroad cars. Several days went by before he left Hopewell for Glenview.

Before Charles Vorhees and Matlick went to the Glenview police, they gathered up Helen Brach's automatic writings and some old diaries of hers and burned them in the furnace of the Glenview home. Charles later told investigators that the papers were full of information that "Helen wouldn't want to have other people reading." He claimed to have a note from Helen with the diaries that said, "Burn these in case something happens to me." He also burned the note, Charles said.

Once Charles Vorhees had filed a missing-person report, the investigation into Helen's disappearance began. Almost three weeks had gone by since she had been seen by anyone.

The checks with the odd signatures made out to Jack Matlick were one of the first pieces of evidence to occupy the police. When Everett Moore, Mrs. Brach's accountant, looked through the cancelled checks he received from her bank, he knew at once that several had not been signed by her. They looked as if they were forgeries. Moore reported what he had found to the Glenview police. When the police turned the checks over to handwriting experts for examination, they confirmed that the signatures were forgeries.

Since most of the checks were made out to Matlick, the police went to him for an explanation. All the caretaker could do was repeat what he had said earlier, that Mrs. Brach had injured her wrist when closing a trunk and her signature was unusual as a result. Matlick insisted the checks were not forgeries; he had actually seen her sign them, he said.

The police went to the airlines for evidence that Mrs. Brach had taken a flight to Fort Lauderdale. But there was no record that she had ever purchased a ticket. Of course, she could have bought a ticket under an assumed name, but there seemed to be no reason why she would want to do that.

Jack Matlick was cooperative with the Glenview police and allowed them to search the house and grounds for clues, and they did so several times. But their searches produced nothing of any importance.

Some investigators believed that Belton Mouras, founder and head of the Animal Protection Institute, a California-based organization, may have had something to do with Mrs. Brach's disappearance. Mrs. Brach had been very generous toward the Animal Protection Institute, contributing as much as $100,000 a year to the organization. It was thought that the Institute might be one of the principal beneficiaries under the terms of the will Mrs. Brach had written.

But Belton Mouras seemed as eager as anyone in trying to find out what happened to Mrs. Brach. He hired Ernie Rizzo, a local private detective who had been involved in several well-publicized cases for well-to-do clients, to trace Mrs. Brach's movements from the time she left the Mayo Clinic.

One of the first things Rizzo did was to fly to

Fort Lauderdale and visit the apartment Mrs. Brach intended to purchase. When he tried the door to the apartment, he found it unlocked, so he entered. Inside, Rizzo found the packages containing the items Mrs. Brach had purchased at the arcade bath shop in Rochester, Minnesota.

Rizzo then flew to Rochester and questioned the clerk in the store where Mrs. Brach had made the purchases. He also tracked down the cab driver who said he had driven Mrs. Brach to the airport for her flight to Chicago.

By the time Rizzo himself was ready to return to Chicago, he felt certain that Mrs. Brach had flown back to Chicago from Minnesota as she had planned and actually arrived at her Glenview home — but never left there alive. While Rizzo would later pursue several other leads, he believed that Jack Matlick was the key to solving the mystery.

One of the failings in the case, according to Rizzo, was that Matlick was never treated as a suspect. He was permitted to remain in the Brach house, with whatever evidence might have been there.

When the Cook County Grand Jury began its inquiry into the Helen Brach case, it arranged for the Brach house to be searched once again. During the search, Mrs. Brach's will was discovered.

According to the will, Helen Brach wanted the bulk of her multimillion dollar estate to go to unfortunate cats and dogs. The chief beneficiary was to be the Helen Brach Foundation, a not-for-profit corporation that had been established by

Mrs. Brach several years earlier and that was to be "operated for the prevention of cruelty to animals." Mrs. Brach herself, her brother Charles, and her accountant, Everett Moore, were to serve as directors of the corporation.

Mrs. Brach's relatives and friends received only modest amounts under the terms of her will. For her brother Charles and his family, the will established a trust fund in the amount of $500,000.

As for Jack Matlick, he was to receive a $50,000 annuity policy, which was expected to provide him with an income of from $4,000 to $5,000 for ten years.

Once the contents of the will had been made known, it became pretty obvious to investigators that Helen Brach had not been done away with for her money. As one investigator put it, following the reading of the will: "The case is like Alice in Wonderland — it keeps getting curiouser and curiouser."

The grand jury heard testimony from a variety of witnesses, but nothing of real importance was learned from them. For a time, the news media had settled on Richard Bailey, the fifty-year-old horse trainer who had dated Mrs. Brach, as a prime suspect in the case. Everyone involved in the case looked forward eagerly to his testimony.

"When did you last see Mrs. Brach?" Bailey was asked. "Where did you meet Mrs. Brach for the first time? Do you know if she is alive at the present time? Did you telephone Mrs. Brach from Florida while she was in the Mayo Clinic? Did you ever talk to Mr. Matlick concerning Mrs. Brach's disappearance?" But Bailey would not answer these or any other questions. He said that by so doing, he might possibly incriminate himself, and thus pleaded the constitutional right to remain silent.

In 1994, after several years of investigation, the United States Attorney's office in Chicago brought formal charges against Bailey, saying that he had romanced Mrs. Brach and succeeded in defrauding her of hundreds of thousands of dollars. Bailey, according to federal authorities, had arranged to have Mrs. Brach killed because she threatened to expose him as a con man. Mrs. Brach was only one of many women Bailey was said to have victimized. He denied all of the charges.

At the time federal authorities brought charges against Bailey, Mrs. Brach's disappearance had been a mystery for seventeen years. More than $200,000 in reward money was being offered for "written information leading to the discovery of the whereabouts of Helen Brach, dead or alive, or the disposition of her body." The bulk of the reward money was to be paid out of the proceeds of her estate, estimated to be more than $20 million at the time. Despite the size of the reward, it never generated clues of any value.

One of the biggest problems in attempting to find a solution in the Helen Brach case is that there is no body. If she met with foul play, if she was murdered, what could the killer have done with Mrs. Brach's remains? For almost two months before her disappearance, the temperature in Chicago and the Upper Midwest had not gone above five degrees. The ground was frozen solid for a depth of three feet. A normal burial was out of the question.

Detective Ernie Rizzo speculated that Helen Brach may have been buried in someone else's freshly dug grave. "In twenty-five years, they'll come across her body," he said.

Long before her disappearance, Helen Brach had arranged for her own burial place, a splendid tomb built at the cost of about half a million dollars on a hilltop site in a small cemetery in Unionport, Ohio. The tomb consists of three stone arches supported by tall columns that span a raised platform containing six burial vaults. Helen's husband and her mother and father are already buried there.

The vault she selected for herself is decorated with a sculpted spray of roses tied with a ribbon above the name HELEN MARIE VORHEES BRACH. Mrs. Brach worked diligently on the monument. She went to Vermont to choose the granite, and hired the artisans that created it. It is sad to reflect that it is not very likely she will ever be buried there.

Death of a Big Shot

The son of an immigrant Chicago fruit peddler, Sam Giancana began his underworld career after dropping out of grade school and joining the mob as a wheelman, or getaway driver. He rose rapidly to control the mysterious institution known as "the syndicate," or "Mafia," ruling a three-state empire of some 1,500 mobsters who ran narcotics, gambling, loan-sharking, and other illegal enterprises.

"In the beginning, he was maybe a nice boy," a longtime friend once said of him. "But then he got big and big and big and suddenly he's a big shot. All of a sudden you look one day and Sam is dressed real sharp and there's money in his pockets. And big troubles on his back. But Sam don't care. He's a big shot."

Cruelty and violence were the norm during Giancana's reign. Whenever there was any trouble in the ranks, any hint of disloyalty, Giancana had a simple solution, "Kill him!" he would order. "Get rid of the guy! That solves the problem." From 1957 to 1966, the years of Giancana's rule, there were 79 mob murders, all of which would have needed his stamp of approval.

Years of decline for Giancana began in 1959, when agents of the Federal Bureau of Investigation planted a microphone in the back room of the mob's headquarters, the Armory Lounge in the Chicago suburb of Forest Park. For the next six years, FBI agents listened to private conversations about syndicate operations. Giancana went to jail in 1965 for refusing to answer grand jury questions about the Chicago underworld.

After his release in 1966, Giancana fled to Mexico to escape government questioners. He lived on a high-walled estate near Cuernavaca, but often commuted to a penthouse he kept in Mexico City.

The Mexican government kicked Giancana out after eight years and he returned to Chicago. While he still would be a factor in the syndicate, his influence had been weakened; he was no longer a big shot.

When Giancana arrived in Chicago after the time he spent in Mexico, detectives from the intelligence bureau and police were there to meet him. He was wearing baggy pants and a wrinkled shirt and carried a bathrobe. Tired and unshaven, he scarcely resembled the smooth and confident Giancana of years past. At police headquarters, Giancana was questioned about his contacts and activities, but gave only vague answers.

In the weeks and months that followed, Giancana's life fell into a routine. His fortress-like house in Oak Park, a quiet residential suburb, served as his headquarters. Joe DiPersio, 81, and his wife, had lived there and kept the house exactly the way Giancana had left it. The heavy mahogany furniture was kept polished and dusted. The paintings, hand-painted lamps, and Giancana's collection of fine German porcelain were in their familiar places.

At the rear of the house was a patio surrounded by a tall stockade fence. No one could see through it or over it. The patio area included a vegetable garden and a small golf green where Giancana practiced putting. DiPersio had worked hard to have the green in readiness for his boss.

On most days, Giancana left his house in the morning to conduct business from his car, which was always chauffered by Dominick (Butch) Blasi, his longtime bodyguard. Blasi would stop at pay phones, where Giancana would make his calls, and at coffee shops, where he conducted meetings.

On the days he didn't go out, Giancana usually worked in his garden or met with mob contacts who dropped by to see him. One of his visitors was Joey (Doves) Aiuppa, who was believed to have taken over the syndicate. It was said that Aiuppa was not happy having Giancana on the scene.

Giancana also became occupied with the federal government's Organized Crime Strike Force and the grand jury called into session to hear testimony from Mafia kingpins. One thing that concerned the grand jury was the late Dick Cain, a onetime Chicago police officer who quit the force and became involved with the syndicate. Cain, who had worked for Giancana in Mexico, was shotgunned to death in 1973 while back in Chicago on a mission for Giancana. Cain's murder had never been solved.

In testifying before the grand jury, Giancana spoke at length but told investigators nothing that they didn't already know. One Strike Force investigator said Giancana had given them nothing but "garbage."

To entice something meaningful from Giancana, the government decided to grant him immunity, meaning he would not be prosecuted on the basis of any information he might reveal. The questioning continued.

Giancana had told close friends that he would do anything "to keep from rotting in jail." When his Mafia associates heard this, they started wearing very worried looks, for they believed that Giancana might eventually crack and start giving the grand jury "real" information.

Giancana was also believed to have fallen out of favor with the syndicate because he wanted to have his authority restored. He wanted to be a big shot again, getting the same payoffs.

But Giancana no longer had the bargaining power he once had. Most of his old associates, the enforcers he had used to maintain his rule, were dead or in jail. He was like a general with no army. The younger element of the Mafia, the "young Turks," as the newspapers called them, had no fear of Giancana. It wasn't like the old days. When Giancana pushed, the young Turks pushed back.

In May 1975, Giancana was visiting a friend in

California when he began suffering severe stomach pains. He insisted on being taken to the Methodist Hospital in Houston, Texas, where surgery was performed to remove his gall bladder.

Giancana remained in the hospital for three weeks. He finally returned home early in June. Weak and thin, he did little but sit around the house.

In mid-June, Giancana's condition was such that he had to return to Houston for treatment and was forced to spend a week there. On June 19, 1975, when Giancana returned to Chicago, Butch Blasi met him at the airport and drove him home.

Agents of the FBI and Chicago's Police Intelligence Division put a tail on Giancana and staked out his home. They had been tipped off that there was to be a welcome-home party for Giancana the next day. That information proved correct. The officers watched as several of Giancana's relatives and mob cronies came and went.

Among those who called on Giancana were Charles (Chuckie) English, a jukebox racketeer and gambling chief, and a trusted friend of Giancana's, and Butch Blasi, Giancana's longtime chauffeur and bodyguard.

Also present that evening were Giancana's daughter, Francine, and her husband, Jerome DePalma, and their daughter. DePalma had accompanied Giancana from Houston. Investigators later learned that DePalma's American Express credit card had been used to pay Giancana's hospital bill.

That evening, Giancana and his five guests

enjoyed a dinner of chicken, baked potatoes, vegetables, and salad. They talked about Giancana's health and assorted family matters.

English and Blasi were the first to leave. Around 10 P.M., the DePalmas left. They got into their car and backed out of the driveway. As they were pulling away, they saw a familiar car approaching. It was Blasi. Why was he returning? Nobody seems to know. The DePalmas exchanged friendly greetings with Blasi, then drove off. Blasi pulled his car into Giancana's driveway and went into the house.

All of this was observed by the detectives who were watching Giancana's house. They also took note of a car that pulled out of the alley on the other side of the house. Unfortunately, the detectives were not able to get a complete license-plate number for that car.

In an upstairs bedroom of Giancana's house, his handyman, Joe DePersio, 81, and his wife watched "The Tonight Show" on television. Around 10:30 DePersio yelled down the stairs to see whether Giancana needed anything. Giancana said no. DiPersio returned to the TV, shutting the bedroom door so as to keep in the cool air from the window air conditioner.

In the yard outside, detectives Howard McBride and Kenneth Hauser decided to make a final check of the premises. They left their unmarked car and began to circle the house on foot. As they approached the rear of the house, they heard several muffled explosive sounds. "Sounds like someone's popping open a couple of cans of beer," said

McBride. The two officers listened for more activity, but heard nothing.

"The house is as dark as a graveyard," said McBride. "Let's call it a night." Hauser agreed. The two detectives went back to their car and returned to headquarters to make their report.

What McBride and Hauser didn't know was that sometime before midnight Giancana went down into the basement kitchen. He was wearing brown pants, a blue-and-white checked sport shirt, and black slippers. Giancana got out a couple of pans. In one, he began to cook some sausage. In the other, he boiled escarole and beans, preparing a meal he would never eat.

At the time, Giancana had a guest. Perhaps he was one of those who had visited earlier, and returned. Or it may have been that Giancana was joined by a new visitor. In either case, whoever was there was surely someone Giancana knew and trusted.

Giancana bent over the stove, poking the sausages as they sizzled in the pan. His guest watched. He could feel the metal of a .22 pistol against his waist.

As Giancana cooked, his guest, moving quickly, slipped up behind him, pulled the pistol from his belt, pressed the barrel against the back of Giancana's head, and squeezed the trigger. A silencer killed the sound. Giancana fell to the floor.

The killer stood over Giancana's body and fired six more times. As blood poured from Giancana's wounds, the killer went through his pockets and pulled out his wallet. He searched through it, then tossed it aside, not taking the credit cards or the $1,458 in cash it contained.

Then the killer fled, leaving through the basement door, out into the warm spring night. He got into his car and drove away, feeling confident that he had not been seen or heard.

Investigators believe the killer threaded his way through the streets of Oak Park and then crossed into River Forest, another suburban community. Suddenly, he heard the whine of police-car sirens. Someone had reported a burglary in River Forest and squad cars from three towns had responded. The killer checked his rearview mirror to see whether any cars were on his trail. His heart was pounding. What if one of the squad cars stopped him and the cops began to ask questions?

The killer pulled over to the side of the road, rolled down the window, and tossed the gun into a grassy stretch next to the road. Then he drove away.

Back at Giancana's house, Joe DiPersio was preparing to retire for the evening. He called down to Giancana one more time to see whether his boss wanted anything. When he got no response, DiPersio went downstairs. He saw Giancana lying face-up on the kitchen floor and he saw the blood. Several .22 caliber shell casings were on the floor around the body. Giancana's wallet was on the floor, too. DiPersio turned off the gas burners and then called an ambulance.

Within minutes, the house was swarming with

Oak Park police and reporters. The Chicago police and federal investigators were not contacted until the next morning, which gave the killer's trail several hours to cool.

When Giancana's three daughters heard the news, they rushed to the scene. Antoinette became hysterical when she saw her father's body. "He's gone! He's dead! My father is dead!" she cried. Her screams were heard by the neighbors, some of whom left their homes to gather in front of the Giancana home to watch the comings and goings of the police and reporters.

The next day, when detective McBride heard the news of Giancana's murder, he realized he and his partner had probably heard the fatal shots, but had mistaken them for the sound made when soda or beer cans are opened.

That summer, the murder weapon — a .22 caliber automatic pistol with a silencer — was found in a ditch in River Forest by a worker mowing grass. Agents of the Treasury Department's Bureau of Alcohol, Tobacco and Firearms were able to trace the weapon to a pair of Chicago police officers who had been manufacturing and selling illegal silencers to local mobsters.

Only a few days after the assassination, Giancana's name was in the headlines again in connection with a Senate committee's hearings in Washington. The committee, which was investigating the Central Intelligence Agency and other government intelligence-gathering agencies, called Johnny Roselli as a witness. A onetime associate of

Giancana's, Roselli told the committee how the CIA had recruited Giancana in 1960 to aid in the assassination of Cuban dictator Fidel Castro.

Giancana had also been scheduled to appear before the Senate committee. This gave rise to the theory that the CIA, fearing what Giancana might say, had sent a hitman to silence him.

After the killing, investigators removed Giancana's desk, filing cabinet, and safe from his home, hoping their contents might provide clues to his killer. Among their discoveries was a carefully detailed chart of Giancana's bets at the race track in 1952. He kept all of the tickets for all of his losing wagers and maintained a list of all of his winners.

Investigators were astonished by how well Giancana had done at the track. His records indicated he had won better than seventy percent of all his wagers, a spectacular showing. His profits amounted to tens of thousands of dollars.

Giancana enjoyed being in the limelight, liked to see his picture in newspapers or magazines. In his desk, detectives found pictures of his daughters with such entertainers as Frank Sinatra, Jerry Lewis, and Dean Martin. There were also photographs of Giancana with singer Phyllis McGuire, who had been his girlfriend.

Some of the items found were of a religious nature. There was a photograph of Giancana with the late Pope Pius XII and half a dozen rosaries, two of them made of gold. The religious articles also included a small bottle of water from the River Jordan.

Several times, Chicago police said they were close to naming Giancana's killer. But they never did.

For a time, Chuckie English, who had called upon Giancana the day of his murder, ranked as the chief suspect. Detective McBride, who was on duty outside of Giancana's home that night, was "absolutely convinced" that English was the assassin.

With an arrest record going back to 1933 for robbery, hijacking, and murder, the seventy-year-old English had once been Giancana's second-in-command. He also supervised syndicate gambling and vending machine operations on Chicago's North Side.

Whether or not English was guilty will never be known, for he was killed on February 9, 1985. He was getting into his Cadillac in a restaurant parking lot in Elmwood Park, just outside of Chicago, when two men wearing ski masks walked up and shot him in the head.

It was believed by many mob-watchers that English was killed because he had fallen out of favor with the syndicate. Or perhaps English really was Giancana's executioner. In that case, a loyal friend of Giancana's might have murdered him to even the score. The police never found English's murderer.

English, Cain, and Giancana had all died in the

same manner that many of their friends and enemies had died: by gangland assassination. "They all die the same way," said a boyhood friend of Giancana's. "Alone. You knew Sam would go this way, you knew it a long time ago, in the old neighborhood."

Another feature of such crimes is that they are very rarely solved. The syndicate is often free to go about its business, without interference, which includes the freedom of handing out its form of justice. To put it plainly, the mob often gets away with murder. It was true in the case of Chuckie English and Dick Cain. Certainly it was also true in the case of Sam Giancana.

"Remember the *Maine*!"

Not long after 9:30 P.M. on Tuesday evening, February 15, 1898, the American battleship *Maine* was blown to pieces in the harbor of Havana, Cuba, bringing death to 260 of its crew members. Was the explosion accidental or deliberately caused? Now, almost a century later, there is no clear answer.

Warships, which have been described as "floating powderkegs," had blown up before the *Maine*, and such disasters have occurred several times since. But none produced effects so far-reaching as when the *Maine* exploded mysteriously in Havana harbor, for the tragedy was enough to start a war.

The war was a brief conflict between the United States and Spain. It was a war that William McKinley, President of the United States at the time, didn't want, and a war the Spanish people didn't want, either. But there were many important interests that did want it, including powerful daily newspapers.

This was a time, after all, before the electronic media, before radio and television. People relied on daily newspapers as their chief source of news and other information, which meant they had enormous influence.

William Randolph Hearst, who published the *New York Journal*, and Joseph Pulitzer, publisher of the *New York World*, were the two leading newspaper czars of the day. They had learned from their coverage of the Civil War that war headlines sold newspapers. So they printed sensational accounts of the Spanish-American War and the events leading up to it, including the destruction of the *Maine*.

Textbooks say the reason the United States went to war with Spain was to "liberate" Cuba, a Spanish colony. For decades, Spain had been struggling to keep control over a native population in Cuba that demanded its freedom. It was a situation similar to the one that had taken place a little more than a century before, when Americans had demanded and won their freedom from England.

While thousands of Cubans had died in the fighting, American newspapers greatly exaggerated the number of casualties, saying that a quarter of the Cuban population had died. The *New York Journal*, in particular, hailed the Cuban rebels as heroes and demanded the United States become involved.

Despite Spain's efforts to end the rebellion, the fighting and rioting continued. President McKinley came to see the unrest as a threat to the many Americans living in Cuba and to American investments there. In an effort to protect American citizens and interests, McKinley decided to send the battleship *Maine* to Cuba.

At the time, the *Maine* was at Key West, the island city some ninety miles due north of Havana at the southern tip of the Florida Keys. Although designated a "Second Class Battle Ship," the *Maine* was as powerful as any American warship afloat, boasting four 10-inch guns, a half-dozen 6-inch guns, and four deck torpedo tubes.

Launched in 1890 at the Brooklyn Navy Yard, the *Maine* could carry over 800 tons of coal in its bins, or "bunkers," coal that was used to feed its eight boilers. All that coal gave the *Maine* a cruising range of some 7,000 miles at speeds of up to 17 knots (between 19 and 20 miles per hour). A crew of 355 officers and enlisted men was needed to operate the vessel.

In the original design for the ship, it was intended that the *Maine* would be able to hoist sails to extend the ship's cruising range. But the use of sails was discarded in the ship's final plans. Having decided to rely on coal rather than wind for its ships, the Navy established a series of coaling stations at various ports. One such coaling station was located at Key West.

In appearance, the 324-foot vessel (less than half the size of a World War II battleship) was dominated by a pair of tall stacks amidships and even taller masts near the bow and stern. The *Maine*'s hull was painted white and the stacks and masts were a light yellowish brown.

On Sunday, January 23, several other ships arrived in Key West to join the *Maine*. They included the battleships *New York*, *Indiana*, *Iowa*, and *Massachusetts*. The next day, the vessels sailed for the Dry Tortugas, some sixty miles to the west, the winter "drill ground" for the Navy's North Atlantic Squadron. Captain Charles Sigsbee, the captain of the *Maine*, expected the ship would be involved in maneuvers with the other vessels until some time in February, when the *Maine* was scheduled to steam for New Orleans for the Mardi Gras celebration.

But President McKinley abruptly changed the *Maine's* schedule. On the night of January 24, Captain Sigsbee aboard the *Maine* received a message from the battleship *New York*, which was serving as the flagship of the fleet, ordering him to come aboard. There he was greeted by Admiral Montgomery Sicard, commander of the fleet, who showed him a message that had just been received from Secretary of the Navy John Long. The message read: "Order the *Maine* to proceed to Havana, Cuba, and make a friendly call. Pay respects to authorities there. Particular attention must be paid to the usual interchange of civilities."

When he returned to the *Maine*, Sigsbee ordered preparations to be made for the ship's immediate departure. Not long before midnight, the anchor was hauled up and the *Maine* began steaming for

Havana. Since Sigsbee did not want to be accused of sneaking into the harbor under the cover of darkness, he cruised slowly so as to arrive after daybreak.

As the ship approached the narrow channel leading to Havana's inner harbor, the crew gazed fearfully at Morro Castle on the eastern shore, a historic fortress whose guns were capable of blasting the *Maine* out of the water. On the other side was Havana itself, with its office buildings, hotels, and the Governor's Palace. Crowds had begun to gather behind a seawall to watch the *Maine*'s arrival.

Steaming into Havana, Captain Sigsbee didn't know what to expect. There were rumors that the harbor had been sown with mines, explosive charges designed for destroying ships. And not long before his departure for Cuba, Captain Sigsbee had been warned by Captain French E. Chadwick of the battleship *New York*, "Look out that those fellows over there don't blow you up."

So it was that Captain Sigsbee was relieved to see a pilot boat approaching, which he took as "evidence of good will." The boat delivered a harbor pilot who guided the *Maine* to a barrel-shaped mooring buoy east of the Navy yard. Sailors fixed a heavy chain from the *Maine* to a ring atop the buoy, allowing the vessel to swing freely, according to the winds and tides. Once the ship was moored, Captain Sigsbee ordered the *Maine*'s guns to boom out a salute to the flag of Spain.

Captain Sigsbee fully realized that his ship, moored to its buoy, was a sitting duck, open to attack from every point of the compass. In an effort to ward off trouble, he got the vessel into a state of battle readiness. The main and secondary gun batteries were supplied with ammunition, and night and day crews were organized to man the guns. Rifles were brought up onto the main deck and ammunition belts were filled with cartridges. A landing party was organized in case orders came to evacuate American citizens from the mainland.

Captain Sigsbee also announced there was to be no shore leave for the 350 crew members. He did not want to take the chance that some merrymaking sailor might create a problem.

On Tuesday, Captain Sigsbee called upon Consul-General Fitzhugh Lee, the American representative in Havana. Later in the week, he made a formal visit to the Cuban Governor-General Parrado. Sigsbee observed that the Cuban leader had received him "with great courtesy."

Captain Sigsbee also opened his vessel to the men, women, and children of Havana. The visitors were impressed by the size of the *Maine*, and the ship's huge guns filled them with awe.

While most Cubans and Spanish seemed to take the sight of the *Maine* in stride, in some the ship stirred deep hatred. One day, a ferryboat passed close to the *Maine* and the passengers jeered at crew members on deck.

And in the city of Havana, flyers were being handed out that referred to the Americans as "Yankee pigs" who had humiliated the Spanish by sending the *Maine* into Havana harbor. "Long live

Spain!" said one of the handbills, "Death to Americans!"

After several days, officers of the *Maine* were permitted to go ashore for sightseeing. Americans in Havana greeted them warmly, but most Spanish kept their distance. To be friendly with the Americans could be taken as evidence that one supported the rebel cause. Even Cuban shopkeepers were aloof.

One afternoon, Captain Sigsbee and several of his officers attended a bullfight at the Plaza de Toros. The captain was not a bullfighting fan especially, but he wanted to test "the feeling of the people of Havana toward the *Maine*." Unfortunately, he didn't get his wish. The people who jammed the stadium were excited and tense, not because of the presence of Captain Sigsbee and his officers, but because of what was happening in the bullring. The party from the *Maine* left before the finish to avoid the crowds.

On Sunday, February 13, Clara Barton, the Massachusetts schoolteacher who had founded the American Red Cross, was invited to lunch aboard the *Maine*. Seventy-five years old at the time, she was in Havana because the Red Cross was handling volunteer relief for Cubans. Barton inspected hospitals and organized food distribution. During her visit aboard the *Maine*, crew members went through a deck drill to entertain her and she chatted pleasantly with the officers about her relief work in Cuba. Before returning to the mainland, she said the Red Cross was standing by to help the

Maine, should its help ever be needed.

For three weeks, the *Maine* rested at its mooring, with the tropical sun beating down. For the crew, in their cramped, stuffy quarters, the stay had become an ordeal. But everyone was thankful that the time had passed peaceably, with scarcely a hint of trouble.

The evening of February 15 was hot and quiet, just as all the others had been. One thing was different, however. The *Maine* had swung to a different position at its mooring. As the ship now lay, its main guns were trained on the city and its shore fortifications. No one aboard the vessel seemed to find any significance in this, however.

At day's end, the ship's bugler sounded "Taps" for lights out. The crew members settled down for the night in their hammocks. The ship grew quiet. Captain Sigsbee was at his desk writing a letter to his wife.

Suddenly, the *Maine* was wracked by a pair of explosions. The first sounded like one of its guns had been fired, but the second, immediately after, was a massive blast that tore the ship apart and sent a cloud of debris and black smoke high above the harbor. The lights went out and then came shrieks and groans from men in pain.

Captain Sigsbee felt his way out of his cabin and started up a passageway leading to the main deck. All of a sudden, he collided with Private William Anthony, his Marine orderly, who told him the ship was sinking.

Captain Sigsbee followed Anthony out onto the main deck. A fire had broken out amidships. From its light, Captain Sigsbee could see that both stacks had been toppled and the bow was a mass of twisted wreckage.

Crew members who had survived the blast were working frantically to get the ship's boats into the water, but only three of the fifteen were fit to be used. The deck on which the captain and the crew members stood was now only a foot above the water's surface. From the shore, dozens of Spanish hurried to get rescue boats to the scene.

Scores of men struggled in the water near the burning wreck. "Help me! Save me!" some cried. Boats steered through the floating debris toward the calls for help. Other floating men were dead or unconscious.

Captain Sigsbee did not want to leave the ship. Then he was told that flames were menacing a powder and ammunition storage area. "Captain, we'd better leave her," said one of Sigsbee's officers. Sigsbee could only agree. "Get into the boats, gentlemen," he said. Sigsbee was able to step over the side into his boat without getting his feet wet.

As the rescue operations continued, the *Maine* settled to the harbor bottom with a great hissing of steam.

The *Alfonso XII*, a Spanish warship, and the *City of Washington*, a big steamship, happened to be moored nearby, and many of the *Maine's* survivors ended up on one of those two vessels. The dining room on the *City of Washington* was turned into a hospital ward, with injured men placed on mattresses on the floor.

Others of the injured were taken to hospitals in Havana, where they were visited by Clara Barton. She was horror-stricken by what she saw. She noted that the men were "bruised, cut, burned; they had been crushed by timbers, cut by iron, scorched by fire, and sometimes blown high in the air . . ."

Captain Sigsbee visited the injured men aboard the *City of Washington* to be sure that they were being cared for properly. Afterward he stood for a few moments on the deck, gazing at the smoking hulk of the *Maine*, a portion of which remained above the surface.

It was not until the next day that an approximate count of the casualties could be made. Many men were missing and thought to be trapped within the wreckage, but it was obvious that some two-thirds of the crew, some 240 men, had perished. Bodies floated ashore for days after the explosion and several survivors died of their injuries, raising the number of fatalities to 260. One observer called it "a wholesale murder of sleeping men."

What caused the disaster? From the beginning, opinion was sharply divided. Many naval officers thought the explosion was accidental. They suspected a bunker in which coal was stored had set itself on fire, a condition known as spontaneous combustion. A pile of oily rags, for example, will sometimes break into spontaneous flame. The spontaneously caused fire in the coal bunker aboard the *Maine* spread to a powder or ammunition storage area, which triggered the explosion.

To others, including most of the newspaper publishers of the day, there was nothing accidental about what had happened. William Randolph Hearst heard about the disaster not long before midnight on Tuesday evening. The night editor of the *Journal* told him the *Maine* had blown up in Havana harbor and the story was being featured on the front page along with "other big stories."

"There is no other big news," Hearst declared. "Please spread the story all over the page. This means war!" CRUISER *MAINE* BLOWN UP IN HAVANA HARBOR was the *Journal's* headline the next day.

By Thursday, the *Journal* was telling its readers the Spanish were responsible. DESTRUCTION OF THE WARSHIP *MAINE* WAS THE WORK OF AN ENEMY, the *Journal* cried. Beneath the headline was a sketch of the *Maine* moored over a mine. The story explained that the mine was linked through a wire to a triggering mechanism at a shore station. The paper called it "an enemy's infernal machine."

That evening another *Journal* headline blared: WAR! SURE! *MAINE* DESTROYED BY SPANISH! The accompanying story explained that salvage divers working next to the *Maine's* hull at the point where the explosion had taken place had found steel plates bent inward. This was clear-cut proof, said the paper, that an explosive device planted outside the ship had caused the blast. If it had been an internal explosion, the plates would have been bent outward.

Captain Sigsbee was practically certain the *Maine* had been blown up by a mine or a torpedo, the *Journal* reported. In this regard, the newspaper was close to the truth. Captain Sigsbee believed the *Maine* had been directed to a mooring site where mines had been planted that could be fired by remote control, somewhat as the *Journal* had described.

The Spanish, meanwhile, opened an investigation into the cause of the disaster. While Captain Sigsbee gave them the plans of the *Maine*, and offered to help them in any way he could, he refused their request to send divers to the site. Nevertheless, the Spanish went ahead with their investigation, which concluded that the explosion had originated inside the ship.

This conclusion was easy to understand. After all, for the Spanish to say a mine had destroyed the *Maine* would have been to risk war with the United States. Spain had little to gain from such a conflict, and much to lose.

Much more attention was focused upon the U.S. Navy's investigation of the disaster. Salvage divers, after spending hours in the water inspecting the *Maine*'s hull, testified before the Navy's board of inquiry. One, a diver from the battleship *New York*, described how he had descended to the harbor bottom and crawled through the mud at the ship's side until he came to the gaping hole caused by the blast. Raising his lantern and peering intently, he found the jagged edges of the steel hull plates to be bent inward, which seemed to indicate a mine had caused the explosion.

The presiding judge, realizing the importance of the diver's testimony, said, "You must be very careful when you say the edge was turned inboard."

"My opinion is, I believe she was blown up from the outside," the diver said, "because no explosion from the inside could make a hole like that."

In its final report, the court of inquiry stated that there had been two explosions aboard the *Maine*, "with a very short and distinct interval between them." The first, said the court, resulted from "the explosion of a mine sitting under the bottom of the ship." This explosion, in turn, caused two ammunition storage areas to blow up.

That was what the papers had been waiting to hear. REMEMBER THE *MAINE*! TO HELL WITH SPAIN! read a headline in the *New York Journal*. The *New York World* demanded that Navy warships be sent to Cuba to bombard Havana. Even the *New York Herald*, which had taken a much calmer view of all that had happened, came out in support of the warmongers. "It is no longer time for debate, but for action," said the *Herald*.

The United States, blaming the Spanish for the explosion, declared war on Spain as of April 21, 1898. "Remember the *Maine*!" became the nation's battlecry.

The first military action in the Spanish-American War took place not in Cuba but in Manila Bay in the Philippine Islands. There the U.S. Navy's

Asiatic Squadron destroyed the entire Spanish fleet.

Military action in Cuba was just as successful. After the American fleet blockaded Santiago Harbor, the army landed some 15,000 troops at Daiquiri and moved toward Santiago. As soon as Santiago came under siege, the Spanish fleet sought to flee Santiago Harbor. Waiting American vessels either sank or forced the beaching of every Spanish ship. Not long after, the city of Santiago surrendered. The war was over by August.

After peace negotiations, Spain agreed to withdraw from Cuba and hand over to the United States both Puerto Rico and Guam, an island in the Marianas, some 2,500 miles west of Hawaii. Spain later sold the Philippine Islands to the United States for $20 million. What Secretary of State John Hay called "that splendid little war" lasted only a few months and put the United States on the road toward superpower status.

The *Maine* was not forgotten. Assistant Secretary of the Navy Theodore Roosevelt, who was to become the nation's president in 1901, had suggested the money be appropriated to raise the *Maine* from the bottom of Havana harbor. This would enable the damaged hull to be studied so that the reason for the explosion could be clearly fixed. In addition, the Cuban government wanted the wreckage removed because it was a hazard to navigation in Havana harbor.

There was another reason, even more important. The remains of approximately seventy members of the crew were still trapped in the wreck. Private groups called for the recovery of the bodies so they could be suitably buried.

In May 1910, work got underway to raise the *Maine* and resink it in deeper water. Engineers built a watertight barrier of steel pilings around the wreckage. Called a cofferdam, it was shaped like an enormous bathtub, 400 feet in length. The water was pumped out of the cofferdam. At the bottom, lay the wreckage of the *Maine*, covered with muck, seaweed, and marine encrustations.

President William Howard Taft appointed a five-man Naval Board of Inspection and Survey to study the wreckage. The board concluded that there had been two explosions (which didn't come as news to anyone). The first was caused by a mine that had gone off outside the hull. This produced a bigger explosion within the ship's ammunition storage areas. These explosions, said the board, "resulted in the destruction of the vessel."

This did not end the controversy. Many experts in ship construction took issue with the Board's findings. The question of what really happened to the *Maine* continued to be debated in the decades that followed.

As recently as 1976, the Navy conducted an investigation of the available evidence concerning the *Maine*. Admiral Hyman G. Rickover, the Navy's highly respected expert on nuclear submarines, headed the study. He and his investigators declared the explosion that destroyed the *Maine* was accidental, and that spontaneous combustion in a coal bunker created enough heat to cause an explosion in an adjacent powder storage area.

The power of the explosion caused the steel plates to bend in different ways. The initial blast could have pushed aside tons of water beneath the ship. The returning rush of the water, said the final report, could have caused the steel plates to bend inward, making it look like there had been a blast from the outside.

Admiral Rickover concluded: "There was no evidence that a mine destroyed the *Maine*."

Early in 1912, after the *Maine* had been refloated inside the cofferdam, preparations were made for the battered vessel's final voyage. Workmen had already recovered the skeletal remains of sixty-six victims of the explosion from the muck and twisted wreckage. These and any personal effects that were found were placed in individual coffins, which were to be brought back to the United States aboard the battleship *North Carolina*.

An opening was cut in the cofferdam, and a trio of powerful tugs then slowly towed the wreck of the *Maine* into deep water several miles beyond the entrance to Havana harbor. A work party was put aboard, and the men opened valves that allowed sea water to flood in. Instantly, the *Maine* started to go down.

The work party was taken off the wreck and before long the stern of the ship lifted into the air and the *Maine* plunged to the bottom. Was the

Maine the victim of a tragic accident — a fire in a coal bin that touched off a massive explosion — or was the vessel blown apart by a Spanish mine? Apparently, the *Maine* carried the answer to that question to its final resting place.

Who Killed
Karyn Kupcinet?

Lovely Karyn Kupcinet went to Hollywood to seek roles in television and films after appearing in stage productions in Chicago, where she was born. Her father was Irv Kupcinet, long-time gossip columnist for the Chicago *Sun-Times*. On the last day of November in 1963, Karyn was found murdered in her Hollywood apartment. She was twenty-two years old.

Except for an overturned coffeepot and a goblet she used as a cigarette holder, there were no signs of a struggle. "She knew her killer, no question about it," said Lieutenant George Walsh of the Los Angeles County sheriff's office. "She would never have opened the door to a stranger."

In seeking to solve the case, police were hampered by Karyn's enormous popularity. "This girl had more friends than anybody I ever heard of," said Lieutenant Walsh, "and they all loved her." Many of her friends were questioned by police during the investigation.

Another complication was the fact that in the

weeks before the crime, Karyn apparently sent threatening notes to her boyfriend and herself. This development bewildered police, complicating the investigation.

Who killed Karyn Kupcinet?

The police don't know for sure. "After more than a quarter of a century of agony, that question still haunts us," says Irv Kupcinet, who, in 1993, at the age of eighty, celebrated his fiftieth year of writing his popular column.

Born on March 6, 1941, Karyn Kupcinet was a plump little girl who was nicknamed Cookie. She attended the exclusive Francis Parker School in Chicago and went on to become a drama major at Pine Manor College in Wellesley, Massachusetts. She continued to have a problem with her weight, and once gained twenty-four pounds in one semester. "I was Miss Five-by-Five," she once told a reporter. But since she had dreams of becoming an actress, Karyn went on a strict diet and got her weight down to 105 pounds. She made her professional acting debut in the Chicago production of *The Anniversary Waltz.*

After college, Karyn enrolled at the famous Actors Studio in New York before heading for Hollywood. She started out by appearing in small theatrical productions, earning praise from the critics for her portrayal of Anne Sullivan in the Laguna Beach Summer Theater production of *The Miracle Worker.*

Little by little, she began getting television roles. By 1963, she had appeared on *The Donna Reed*

Show, *Surfside Six*, *Hawaiian Eye*, and, most recently, *Perry Mason*. She also had a small role in Jerry Lewis's film *The Ladies Man* and more than a dozen stage roles to her credit.

Late in November that year, Karyn had written to her parents in Chicago, telling them she was excited over the prospects of an upcoming trip to Palm Springs. On Friday evening, November 29, they telephoned her in Hollywood, but got no answer. "She's probably out," Irv Kupcinet said to his wife. "We'll try tomorrow."

Two of Karyn's closest friends, Mark Goddard, 27, and his 25-year-old wife, Marcia, had also tried calling Karyn that Friday, and got no answer. When they tried her again on Saturday night and the telephone again went unanswered, the couple decided to go over to Karyn's apartment and check on her. Karyn lived near Sunset Strip in an eighteen-unit apartment complex that was occupied mostly by TV and motion picture performers.

Outside the door of Karyn's apartment on the second floor, the Goddards saw daily newspapers from the previous three days, two magazines, and a copy of Henry Miller's *Tropic of Cancer*. The book seemed to have been placed there by someone who didn't find her at home. There was a small Christmas wreath on the door.

Mark Goddard peered in one of the windows. No one seemed to be home. When there was no answer to the doorbell, the Goddards tried the door, found it unlocked, and entered. The apartment was dark. "We called her name — 'Karyn!

Karyn!' — and thought she might be asleep because the TV was on," Goddard was to say later. Then they turned on the lights, and gasped. Karyn was lying on the couch, face down. They knew at once she was dead.

The Goddards called another tenant in the apartment complex who contacted the sheriff's office. Soon Karyn's apartment was swarming with deputies. They noted an empty coffee pot and a small glass overturned on the floor. Close by were a spoon, a small pillow, and a stuffed pink and white panda.

In searching the apartment, investigators found several bottles of pills in the bathroom medicine cabinet, which were taken to the police laboratory for analysis. There were no notes in the apartment, nothing to indicate Karyn may have committed suicide. "Karyn was very vivacious and happy the last time we saw her," Mark Goddard told a reporter. "She was not the sort of girl who would commit suicide."

Back in Chicago, Karyn's mother and father were shocked by the news of their daughter's death. Her father, accompanied by his brother, took the first available flight to Los Angeles. While waiting in the Chicago airport to board the plane, Karyn's sorrowful father sat with his face in his hands, weeping.

An official autopsy on Karyn's body revealed that she had been strangled. The report stated that her death has been caused by "asphyxiation due to manual strangulation." The killer, the medical examiner noted, had used so much force that he had broken a small bone in Karyn's neck. It was also reported that Karyn was killed just before midnight on Wednesday or very early Thursday morning.

The Goddards told police investigators that Karyn had been their dinner guest on Wednesday night. She was expected at 6:30 P.M., said Mark Goddard, who played a detective on the TV series *The Detective*, but showed up about an hour late. She explained that she had been delayed by a telephone call from Andrew Prine, her boyfriend.

When the Goddards and Karyn sat down to eat, Karyn merely toyed with her food and drank nothing. She left the Goddards around 8:30 P.M.

Karyn apparently went straight home. Around 9 P.M., Edward Rubin, a freelance writer who was friendly with Karyn, knocked on her door, and she invited him in. "She seemed bothered by something," Rubin later was to say, "and after a little while, she went out for a walk."

During her walk, Karyn happened to meet actor Robert Hathaway, another friend. Both Hathaway and Rubin had come to know Karyn through Andrew Prine. As Karyn and Hathaway chatted, Karyn told him that Rubin was in her apartment and invited him to go back with her. "We watched television and had a piece of cake and some coffee," Hathaway told investigators. Hathaway and Rubin left Karyn's apartment about 11:15. They were the last people known to have seen Karyn before she was strangled.

In its initial stages, the investigation of the crime concentrated on Karyn's friends. The tall, slender Andrew Prine, who was divorced from actress Sharon Farrell, and who had been co-starring in NBC's *Wide Country*, was brought in for questioning, as were Edward Rubin and Robert Hathaway. Besides being questioned, all three agreed to undergo lie-detector tests.

When Andrew Prine was questioned, he explained that his romance with Karyn was on shaky ground, that he and Karyn had recently agreed not to see so much of one another and not to get too serious. He said that he had telephoned the actress around 6:30 Wednesday evening [just before her dinner with the Goddards] and that they had had a "slight misunderstanding." After the call, Prine went to a movie. He said that when he got home from the movie around midnight, he called Karyn again in an effort to iron out their differences. Prine was thus the last person known to have spoken to Karyn.

Meanwhile, Karyn's grief-stricken father had arrived in Los Angeles. He told a reporter that his daughter was a "bubbling and enthusiastic" young woman and that there was "nothing serious" between Karyn and Andrew Prine. When he made a visit to Karyn's apartment, he walked from room to room without saying a word. He later sadly accompanied his daughter's body back to Chicago.

The funeral service for Karyn at Temple Shalom on Lake Shore Drive in Chicago was attended by more than 1,500 people, including Illinois Governor Otto Kerner and Chicago Mayor Richard Daley. During the services, Karyn was described as a woman "born to be a star."

Back in Los Angeles, when police questioned Andrew Prine a second time, he revealed that both he and Karyn had found strange notes threatening their lives tacked to their front doors not long before Karyn died. The notes were crudely made and consisted of words that had been cut from magazines and newspapers and taped on sheets of plain paper.

One of the notes read:

YOU MAY DIE WITHOUT NOBODY
WINNER OF LONELINESS WANTS DEATH
UNTIL
SOMEONE SPECIAL CARES

Prine, who had kept the notes, originally figured they were the work of some crackpot. But after what had happened to Karyn, the notes suddenly seemed very significant, and Prine turned them over to police.

The notes loomed as the first solid clue to come into the possession of the police. But when police laboratory technicians examined the notes, the investigation took an unexpected turn. Karyn's fingerprint was found on a piece of transparent tape on one of the notes. It was positively identified as the print of Karyn's right middle finger.

Police pointed out the fingerprint could not

have been made by someone handling the notes because it was on the underside of the tape, the "sticky" side.

Could it be possible that Karyn, the murder victim, had composed the notes herself? To find out, police returned to Karyn's apartment and gathered up all the magazines they could find and then went through them page by page. They were chiefly news, fashion, and movie magazines. Just as they had suspected, investigators found that the words used to construct the notes had been cut from the magazines.

Police were dumbfounded. If Karyn had prepared the notes, then what they had considered to be their hottest clue was suddenly worthless.

Police Captain A. W. Etzel believed that the notes were only one of several things that Karyn did in an effort to keep Andrew Prine from breaking up with her. Police investigators discovered she had called Prine shortly before her death and said to him, "Someone left a baby on my doorstep."

Prine told her to call the police and they would tell her what she should do. When they spoke again, Karyn told Prine that she had called the police and they came and took the baby away. But when Etzel checked the files, he could find no record of a baby being turned over to the police. He said he thought the entire incident to be "pure fantasy."

Lie-detector tests given to Karyn's friends and others were inconclusive. Various leads investigators pursued proved worthless. In the end, police were unable to find the person responsible for Karyn's death.

Karyn's father, on the other hand, had his own idea of who might have killed his daughter. In his autobiography, *Kup — A Man, An Era, A City*, published in 1991, the Chicago newsman named David Lange as one who might be the guilty party. Lange lived in the same building as Karyn, occupying an apartment on the first floor just below hers.

On the night of the murder, Kupcinet pointed out, Lange was in his apartment with his girlfriend. He heard the commotion after Karyn's body was discovered and the police were called, the police sirens and the sound of people running up and down the stairs. Lange ignored the excitement and did not leave the apartment to see what was going on, even after someone knocked on the door and told him what had happened.

"Police suspect . . . he chose not to appear on the scene because he already knew what had happened," Kupcinet wrote in his autobiography. "That enabled him to stay clear of authorities."

Kupcinet also said that the police have a statement from a friend of Lange's who reported that he told her that he was the person who killed Karyn. According to his autobiography, Kupcinet is disturbed by what he believes was the failure of the Los Angeles police to follow up on the leads that seemed to point to Lange.

In his book, *Hollywood's Unsolved Murders*, John Austin wrote of Karyn Kupcinet's death. Said

Austin: "Perhaps one day the sheriff's police will come up with a lost clue, a dropped word, a deathbed confession that will lead to the murderer of Karyn Kupcinet."

To these words, Irv Kupcinet added: "That's our only hope at this late date."